WE ARE NOT ALONE IN THE DARK

Copyright © 2024 by Ryan Hoyt

All rights reserved

Published by Machete & Quill Press

Paperback & ebook cover by Matt Seff Barnes

Hardcover art by Eva Mout (ursusart.studio), used under license

Machete & Quill Press logo by Randy Laybourne

No part of this book may be reproduced in any form or by any electronic or mechanical means, including information storage and retrieval systems, without written permission from the author, except for the use of brief quotations in a book review.

All characters, places, and events in this book are fictitious. Any resemblance to actual events or persons, living or dead, is strictly coincidental.

First edition in all formats: 2024

Paperback ISBN: 978-1-956163-13-1

Ebook ISBN: 978-1-956163-12-4

Hardcover ISBN: 978-1-956163-14-8

WE ARE NOT ALONE IN THE DARK

A MACHETE & QUILL HORROR
RYAN HOYT

Machete & Quill Press

Content Warnings

This book contains scenes of bullying and domestic abuse. Reader discretion advised.

If you or someone you know is experiencing domestic abuse, help is available. Please consider contacting the National Domestic Violence Hotline at 1-800-799-7233 in the US or the National Domestic Abuse Helpline in the UK at 0808 2000 247.

If you are experiencing bullying, contact the Stop Bullying Now Hotline (US) at 1-800-273-8255 or Childline (UK) at 0800 1111.

*To the Arbutus & Camellia kids and all our friends.
We were so alive back then.*

Chapter One
BRYAN | OCTOBER, 1991

"If I tell you that the light has a physical presence, I don't think you'll really grasp what I mean. Not the bulb itself, but the actual brightness. It holds me down like glue, as if some illuminated gel fills the room and pins me to my bed.

"I've heard stories of sleep paralysis, how people wake up in the middle of the night and, despite their consciousness, can't send a message to the rest of their body to wiggle a foot or lift a finger. Hopelessness and dread fills them. Panic kicks in, yet nothing changes. Neither the fight nor flight instincts have any control. They're stuck.

"It's just like that when the light comes to my room, stinging my pupils with its intense hue, just before those silhouettes come into view. Their shadows, humanlike in the most basic composition in that they have two legs, two arms, one head, standing upright, and yet in the details revealed even just through those shadows, they are nothing like us at all. Their heads stretched like over-filled balloons, their fingers twisting and fluid like a family of snakes escaping a nest after devouring baby birds.

"I can't pull my blankets up to hide from them. I can't roll off my bed and crawl under. All I can do is watch as they approach me.

"They reach for me. Their fingers slither along my cheeks, my lips, into my nostrils, and a darkness as unwanted as the light overtakes me. What happens after that, I can't tell you. Sometimes little pieces of it are with me when I wake up in my bed the next morning, some foggy memories that dissolve into the air like any normal dream, evading my attempts to pluck them out and hold on to them. I'm left only with a deep feeling of dread. Of disgust. Of hatred toward myself for not fighting back."

"It's completely normal to feel that way after what you've been through."

The voice pulls me from a different kind of daze, one that you find yourself in when you're really invested in a story being told. I feel as if I am watching it play out on television even though I am the storyteller. Doctor Halpert ("Please, call me Pete," he'd said, but I don't want to be his friend.) flashes a smile to tell me that I am safe with him, yet I know exactly what he is thinking behind it.

"You don't believe me," I say, not wanting to play his game.

"Believe in the aliens and the light made of gel? Absolutely not. However, I do believe that *you* believe it, that it was very real to you. I also believe that it stems from—"

"The abuse from my dad," I finish for him. "Of course that's what you think. That's all it ever is with your kind. You're the third shrink the social workers have made me visit, and you're all the same. Screw my dad and what he did to me, sure, but this ain't that. This is what I'm dealing with. You want to get down to the bottom of why I'm falling asleep in class, why I'm short with my temper? It's because I'm not sleeping at night. Whatever these things are, they're doing something to me almost every night, and even though I'm blacked out for most of it, I still wake up every morning feeling like I've been up chugging two-liters all night."

"What you've described is much like veterans from the Vietnam War, Bryan. The things they experienced, the deaths they saw around them, the people they hurt, the pains inflicted on them. It all causes the brain to rewire itself, to change the rules of how it functions, how it perceives reality and mixes it up with fantasy."

"Fantasy?" I can't take another word. My right hand trembles, and all I can think to do at this point is to thrust the hand forward and slap the plastic cup of water off of the coffee table between us. I do it. The water sprays on the wall, but the cup's soft plop onto the rug doesn't satisfy me. I get to my feet and reach for the table. As I lift the edge nearest me, Doctor Halpert leans forward and counters my attempts with his own hands, bringing the table back down on all four legs. "Screw you!" I scream and storm out.

"You know I can't afford to take you to any more appointments, don't you?" Mom asks in the car on the way back to school. I reach for the radio dial, but she slaps my hand down. "I wish you had made the most of them instead of yelling at the doctors every time. We get one free initial appointment before they charge us the hourly rate, and those extra hours cost more than I make in a shift at the diner."

"They never take me seriously, Mom. They just think everything is all about Dad." She tenses up at the mention of him. "I mean, sure, he screwed us up good, but that doesn't mean he still has power over me. He's gone, and that's all that matters."

"So what are we all supposed to believe? That little green Martians are coming and taking you from your room? I'm sorry about Daddy, hon. I hate him for what he did, but—"

"No you don't," I say. Mom flinches as my voice rises, and I despise myself immediately. The power is just like what my dad thought he wielded when he hurt one of us. Yet, I continue with it. "You kissed him in the courtroom when they said he was guilty. You cried when they told us how long he was going to prison for. You still miss him after everything!"

The light turns red. Mom notices late and slams on the brakes, the car skidding to a halt halfway over the crosswalk lines. The truck behind us lays on its horn, but I don't hang around to see how Mom will react. I reach for the handle, open the door, and jump out. We are only a few blocks from school, so I run the rest of the way. She doesn't make any attempt to follow me.

Part of me wants to run back home. Mom had traded shifts with Franny Melville to take me to the appointment, so she'll be at the diner for the lunch and dinner rushes. I'd have the house to myself. The thought of being in that dump alone sours my stomach, though. My bedroom makes me think of the abductions, and the rest of the house reminds me too much of my dad. I like hanging out in the barn, but it's too close to the rest of the house, so back to school it is. My bike is there anyways from when I rode in this morning. I missed third and fourth periods along with lunch for the appointment, so science and gym are all that remain of the day. Not so bad. At least Miss Halsey cuts me slack most of the time.

I sign myself in at the office and grab a pass from the secretary to excuse my tardiness. On the way to the science room, I retrieve my backpack from my locker, wincing at the weight of the textbooks. As I approach the lab, an unfamiliar voice floats out of the open door.

I step in to see a substitute teacher struggling to get the attention of the students.

"It would not behoove me to hand out detentions to each and every one of you," she croaks out in an ancient voice. Her tightly permed hair is white with a tint of purple. She wears khaki shorts that reveal thin legs with saggy skin over her knees, as wrinkled as her face. Her massive glasses are straight out of the seventies, her eyes magnified threefold. With her sunken cheeks, she looks uncannily like a fish out of water, sucking air with desperation. Behind her, *Mrs. Porter* is written on the chalkboard. Twenty minutes into the class period and that is apparently as far as she's gotten with the agenda.

Nobody sits in their assigned seats, and the only chair left is front and center. So much for entering unnoticed. Everyone stops their chit-chatting and watches me patter up to Mrs. Porter. She glances down at the attendance sheet on her clipboard, then back up at me. "And you are?"

"Bryan."

"Bryan?" she asks, scanning the names. "What's your last name?"

"Adams," I respond.

Her eyebrows furrow. She raises her head to face me. "Bryan Adams? We have a celebrity here, ladies and gentlemen. Either that or a comedian." Everyone laughs. Someone belts out the chorus to the love song from the Robin Hood movie. I don't need to turn around to know it's Jason Unger. "Now tell me your real name so I know what to put on the detention slip."

"That is my real name," I insist.

She taps the clipboard with a gnarled arthritic finger. "The only Adams on here is Leslie Adams. Is that you?"

The other kids roar at this. A barrage of spitballs and wads of binder paper pelt me from behind. "Damn, Leslie, you're the nastiest girl here, and that's saying a lot! Woof," Jason Unger shouts from the back of the room. The other kids *ooh*, inviting me to turn around and respond. I ignore it.

"Yes, that's me, but please call me Bryan. It's my middle name." The heat in my face overwhelms me and I can smell the sweat pouring down my arms and back. I plop down on the open chair and avoid looking at the rest of the students. I only have three friends, but they all have gym class this period while I'm stuck with these cretins.

"I think Leslie is a lovely name. When I was a child, I knew several wonderful boys named Leslie." This time the kids make a *woooh* sound, the way the audience does when two characters in a sitcom flirt or kiss on set. Mrs. Porter ignores them as she turns and walks toward the corner of the room where the janitor had left the A/V cart. In other classes, it's always exciting when a teacher plugs in the extension cord attached to that tower on wheels, and the VCR powers on, blinking *12:00*, the TV flashing on with the illuminated snow of channel three.

In science class, however, it just means some boring documentary. This time I groan along with the other students as the substitute starts the video that our teacher left behind.

It's a recording from a PBS program on frog dissections, which seems to perk up half the class and causes the other half to shift uneasily, their still-digesting lunches having second thoughts in their bellies. I didn't eat lunch because I was at my appointment, but that isn't unusual on other days, either. Mac always offers to share whatever his mom packs into his brown bag, and I accept bits and pieces, but that's the extent of my normal lunch. Howard offered a couple of times and I appreciated it, but his lunch is eaten with spoons and forks from Tupperware containers, not easily shared out of wrappers and baggies. Jay is always willing to share, but that boy needs all the food he can get inside of him so he doesn't blow away with the wind.

A collective gross-out groan comes from my classmates, which is when I realize I haven't been paying attention. I focus on the square screen with its brightness dialed up far too high and take in the sight of a croaked frog sprawled out on a tray not unlike the ones in the cafeteria. The host-slash-scientist in his baby-blue lab coat brings his scalpel down against a spot on the frog's exposed underside. He presses down and starts the incision. The groans intensify around the room, and I find myself leaning in. My breath catches in my chest as the camera zooms in on the carnage the scientist creates on that frog's little carcass.

The blade slides down, the body slits open.

A moment of darkness overtakes my vision. Then a light. Bright. Thick. Blinding. I shift my head only slightly, but the effort to move even that much is massive. With the light out of my direct line of sight, I catch a glimpse of my captor, still only a shadow, just on the edge of my vision. Instead of a scalpel, there's some kind of tube in its twisted fingers. The creature's hand comes close to my face. My eyes cross as I attempt to identify what it holds. A bottle of some material neither plastic nor glass. The fingers tighten around the bottle, squeezing its contents into my mouth. I try to clamp my jaw shut, but it's then that I notice something is wedged between my lips to keep me from closing my mouth. A thick, slimy substance lands on my tongue, fills my throat. I try to scream, but only a gurgle escapes me. I take in air through my nose and try again.

My gasp comes out more like a croak, as if I'm imitating one of the frogs in the video.

"Mister Adams!" Mrs. Porter yells from the back of the room as she flips the lights on. "If you cannot be mature in this classroom, you may go and see the principal. Our State Board of Education has deemed frog dissections a necessary learning experience for children of the tenth grade, so I expect more from young men such as yourself."

The class roars with laughter. A tissue box sails

through the air from Jason Unger's corner in the back of the room and slams against my head. I try to speak, to apologize, to offer some excuse about having fallen asleep and having a bad dream, but the bell saves me from further embarrassment. The other kids are out the door, forgetting about me for the moment.

"Are you okay, Leslie?" Mrs. Porter asks as I pass her on my way to the hall. I nod and step through the doorway.

That's when a fist slams into my stomach. I stumble into the lockers just outside the classroom and slink to the floor.

"Are you okay, Leslie?" Jason says in a mocking voice. He spits on my shirt before making his way to his next class. The wad of brown and yellow phlegm stretches like slime and drops to the checkered floor. People stop in the hall to flash looks of pity, but none dare to defend me and get on the school bully's bad side the way I so clearly am.

As terrible as the day has been, I'm still glad it isn't night.

Chapter Two
MAC

Even from behind, the flow of golden liquid was visible between the legs of the ogre standing in the bike cage. Mac Alden watched in disgust as the spray splashed off the seat and red frame of a bicycle.

"He has the intelligence of a dog," Howard Chen said. Mac turned to watch the approach of two friends.

"That's an insult to dogs," Jay Patel added. "Jason is a much lower life form."

Mac grabbed each of his friends' sleeves and pulled them around the corner of the building as Jason turned with a smirk. The bully zipped his jeans before kicking over a couple other bikes in the cage and exiting.

"What are we going to do?" Howard asked.

"I have a full bottle on mine," Mac said. "I'll pour it over the mess before Bryan gets here."

"He's always late from gym anyways," Jay said.

Once Jason was out of sight, the trio jogged through the gate. Mac cut across to his silver bike, which was locked to the chain link fence on the far side of the cage. He reached for the plastic bottle fixed to the frame, only to jerk his hand back. "That's not water!" He turned toward his friends in time to see Jay's eyes widen.

"Look out!" Jay called, but it was too late. As Mac turned, a yogurt cup flew at the fence. It hit its mark, and the contents found their way between the metal grating and splattered all over Mac's face.

Through the drips of coagulated dairy on the fence, he caught sight of Jason and the oaf's oversized middle finger. "Enjoy the snack, Mac. Don't even think about helping your little girlfriend Leslie."

In his frustration, Mac kicked the water bottle on his bike and the lid plopped off. Stale urine splashed out onto the weeds.

"Mine's clean," Jay said of his bike on a center rack. "Howard?"

"My tires are empty but I found the caps. It looks like he just squeezed them out this time instead of slashing the tubes."

Jay uncapped his water bottle and poured it over Bryan's bike. The sixteen ounces of plastic-leeched water didn't make a dent on the stench of piss, but at least their friend would come back to a somewhat cleaner ride than how they'd found it. Howard crouched in the weeds and fished the portable pump out of his backpack. This wasn't the first time, so he'd been prepared. His bag was also well-stocked with new tubes and a pack of wipes. He tossed the wipes to Mac.

"Thanks," Mac muttered as he set to work cleaning the yogurt off his face and shirt. He bunched up another couple wipes to get the pee off his own bike and another wipe to grip the bottle, which he discarded amid the sea of bicycles. Other students came in for their own bikes and glared at the trio as if the stench was their fault. Mac ignored them and crossed over to Bryan's bike to disinfect the seat and frame.

"You guys don't need to hide what happened." Mac turned to find Bryan weaving in between the other students leaving the cage with their own bikes. Bryan's face looked more downcast than usual. "It's not like this doesn't happen at least once a month. Screw that guy."

"Yeah, screw him," Jay chimed in. "Someone ought to knock him down a peg or two. I'd do it, but my doctor said my bones are too fragile to fight."

There was a pause, and then Howard, Bryan, and Mac broke into laughter.

"What?" Jay feigned innocence. He was the smallest of their group by a good four inches. At their age, it may as well have been four feet. He also looked to be under a hundred pounds, though Mac had never seen a day go by where Jay hadn't pounded down slices of pizza for lunch. His parents seemed to have an endless supply of leftover pizza, which he pulled out of his brown paper bag every afternoon, wrapped in foil.

"Let me guess." Bryan wiped away tears from his fit of laughter. "He spared your bike again, Jay?"

"Doesn't he always?" Howard asked.

"I wish Jason's dad worked for *my* dad instead," Mac said.

"Not just worked for. Jay's dad took the man's job and practically spanked him with it," Howard added. They cracked up all over again at this. Jay beamed with pride.

"Hell yeah. My dad is the only one to defeat an Unger in this town so far." Jay's dad was almost a mirror image of the boy, only bald and wrinkled. He was nearly as old as Mac's grandparents. Jay resented his father's genes, though, which had apparently passed down to him. Still, he took pride in this particular accomplishment. When the Patel family moved to town twelve years earlier, the community had lacked a licensed medical doctor. Folks had to drive thirty minutes east to Raventree Hollow or even farther depending on the services they needed. The closest they had in town was Miles Unger, Jason's father. He was a Vietnam War veteran, a medic in the unit he had been assigned to, but he hadn't come back unscarred by the violence he had witnessed in his years overseas. The man was prone to fits of unbridled anger, which Mac guessed was the reason Jason had ended up the way he was. Still, he'd been capable enough to run an unlicensed home visit medical practice for a few years.

When Dr. Patel arrived and opened a medical practice of his own, Miles Unger watched helplessly as the demand for his services dried up. Dr. Patel not only hired him, but also paid for the man's training as a nurse.

"Are we heading to Howard's?" Jay asked as the boys sped away from school. "My mom said you guys are always welcome at my house."

"Let's go to my place," Bryan said. "My mom is working swing shift today so it'll be quiet there." They turned left down the next street and headed for the Adams farm on the outskirts of town.

Mac glanced over at him as the boys pedaled down the road. He could tell Bryan was trying his best to ignore the mess that remained on his bike even after the wipes. Despite that, the look on his face concerned Mac.

"Hey Jay, how about grabbing your laser tag set?" Mac asked.

"But my house is the opposite direction!" Jay pouted.

"It's five minutes, you goon," Howard jested.

"You go with him too, Howard," Mac instructed. Howard started to complain, but Mac's stare was firm.

"Fine," he said, slowing his bike to turn around. "Let's go, Jay. See you guys in a bit." The pair disappeared behind them as Bryan and Mac continued. Bryan looked forward and kept on without a word. The silence would have been awkward with anyone else, but it was at home with Bryan. It was part of him, wrapped around him like a shield, one that had probably hardened after everything he'd gone through as a child.

"Damn it," Bryan said a few minutes later as they winded through the road up to the dilapidated farm he called home. As they crested the one slight rise on the approach to Bryan's house, Mac spotted what had upset his friend. Mrs. Adams's car was parked in the gravel next to the front porch.

"I thought you said she was working late," Mac said.

"Something must have happened. It'll be my fault." He sped ahead, leaving Mac in the dust of the disheveled road.

Mac made no attempt to keep up, knowing that Bryan would need a couple minutes with his mom to warn her that company was on their way. Instead, he hit the brakes and skidded to a halt. He reached for his water bottle to quench his thirst before he remembered what had happened to it. Instead, he engaged the kickstand and left his bike in the road. With Mrs. Adams at home, it was unlikely anyone else would drive this direction any time soon. He looked around, taking in the sight of the once prosperous farm that now looked like an overgrown wasteland. Man-sized weeds sprouted up as far as the eye could see. A grove of fruit trees in the western part of the property grew wild, though most of the fruit rotted on the branch these days. On the east side, just behind the sagging barn, rows of corn stalks flourished, providing an endless supply of meals for seemingly thousands of crows.

The place had been successful within Mac's lifetime. He remembered Bryan's dad as a staple in the weekly farmers' market, there every Saturday and Sunday morning with little Bryan in tow. Mac would always seek out his buddy and they'd run around, hiding under stall tables until Mac's parents would find them and scold them for running off. A couple times, however, Bryan's dad had found them first, and Mac would have liked to forget those moments. The man's temper flared up even in front of his fellow neighbors or children like Mac. He knew none of them would stop him from disciplining his unruly child.

The hinges squeaked as Bryan pushed through his front door and stepped out onto his porch. Mac squinted toward him and saw his friend motioning that it was okay to come in. Mac got back on his bike, raised the kick stand, and started to pedal when he heard laughter behind him. He turned to see Jay and Howard approaching, their backpacks exchanged for a large duffel bag. The boys rode side by side, each holding a handle of the bag that sagged down between them. By the time the three of them pulled up to Bryan's porch, Mrs. Adams was standing beside her son, hands on her hips like your typical angry mother.

"What kind of trouble do you plan on getting into tonight?" she asked as she looked the boys over. Her eyes caught on Howard. "You aren't planning on setting anything on fire this time, are you?"

Mac followed her gaze to Howard, who flushed with

a look of guilt. "No, ma'am," Howard managed. "That was just an accident."

"The firecrackers were mine," Mac admitted. "Howard only lit the one, but he shouldn't have thrown it into the dry grass like that."

"Sorry, ma'am."

Her glare softened as a smile formed on her face. "I'm only messing with you. I know you are good kids." She reached over and mussed Howard's hair. "All of you! Now, my shift got pushed to graveyard, so I'm going to need y'all to take good care of my boy." Bryan's face fell at this. He turned around, threw the screen door open, and stomped into the house. The door slammed shut behind him. Mrs. Adams rolled her eyes. "I don't know what has gotten into him. Anyways, there's junk food in the fridge. Leftover hash browns from the diner and some pie. Enjoy yourselves!"

She walked to her car and drove away as Mac, Jay, and Howard leaned their bikes against the porch and followed their friend inside.

A door slammed upstairs just as they came through the front entrance. "Is it the alien thing or is he in sad-boy mode again?" Jay asked.

"Full sad-boy mode for sure," Howard replied. "Let's see if he puts on a Smiths record and applies eyeliner."

Jay continued with it. "Just to watch the black run down his cheeks as he cries."

Mac rolled his eyes at them and headed upstairs after his best friend.

"We're just playing, Mac," called Howard. "You know he's our best buddy!"

Mac ignored them and continued his ascent. Each step bowed and creaked. How the decrepit farmhouse still stood was beyond Mac's comprehension. Fist-sized holes in the wall remained unpatched even three years after Bryan's dad went to prison.

"I'll be down in a minute," Bryan called through the door before Mac's knuckles rapped on the wood.

"It's just me, dude. The guys are downstairs."

Mac heard Bryan's footsteps patter across the room. The knob turned and his friend stood in the doorway of the dim room, eyes red and wet with tears. Bryan wouldn't have opened the door had Jay or Howard been there; Mac was his oldest friend and the only one he felt okay to be vulnerable around.

"What's going on with you today, Bry?"

"It's been a shitty day, that's all." He turned and walked across the room to sit on his unmade bed. Mac's mom would never have let him go to school in the morning without making his bed and smoothing out any lumps and wrinkles below his comforter, not to mention picking up dirty clothes all over the floor and removing any soiled dishes. Bryan's mom, on the other hand, never had the energy or will to enforce any rules in the Adams household. Mac simultaneously felt jealousy and pity, though he also felt guilty about thinking either way. He pushed off a stack of dirty t-shirts and plopped down on the wooden chair. It had been part of the set in Bryan's dining room but was cast out when an armrest had snapped off during one of his dad's angry fits years ago.

"You weren't at lunch."

"Another stupid therapy appointment. He didn't believe me. They never do."

"About the..." Mac took a deep breath before finishing. "The night visits? I mean, Bryan, can you blame anyone for not believing it?"

"Including you."

"Dude, it's not like that. I want to believe you but listen to what you're saying. I know *you* believe it's real, and that's enough for me, but that doesn't mean it's easy to comprehend."

"So you don't think I'm a lunatic?" Bryan asked. A smile cracked on his face and both boys laughed together, but Bryan's quickly faded. "And then there's Unger."

"Fucking Jason. I hate that guy." Again they cracked up together, this time at the shock of Mac's word choice. His was normally the cleanest mouth of the group, but that bully brought out the worst in everyone.

"Alright, let's get back to the guys before they start making jokes," Bryan said. Mac watched as he stood with confidence, always quick to rebound from hard moments. As Mac rose to his own feet, a chill swept over him. The window was open just a crack. He reached over the desk covered in books, food-stained dishes, and unfinished homework assignments and slid the window shut. He reached for the lever to lock the window, but it moved loosely without catching.

"Bry, the window won't lock."

Bryan stopped at the doorway and turned back. "It never stopped them anyways." Then he disappeared through the doorway and down the stairs.

Chapter Three
BRYAN

The cornstalks slap against my face as I run. Their rough edges scratch at my cheeks when I jump into the next row to evade my pursuers. I ignore any pain as the patter of footsteps in the dirt and detritus gets louder. Closer.

The stench of my own sweat is putrid. That alone could give me away in between rows of stalks if my panting breaths don't do it first. The footsteps draw near, only feet away, perhaps two or three rows over. I hold still and cut off my breathing so as not to make a sound. The footsteps move on up the field.

I release my breath and step through another row to put more distance between us, but I interrupt a crow in its meal. It caws with rage and flies off, sending a signal to the others of my whereabouts. Motion in the stalks behind me. I turn back to see the taller stalks two rows over parting. I pivot my body and make to run, but a stalk already trampled earlier in this pursuit bends outward in my path, catches my foot. I fall to the ground and let out an involuntary *oof* as the wind is knocked from my chest.

I flip around onto my back. A red light hits my chest, then a second. I lift my head to watch.

Pew

Pew

Bloop

Buzz

A vibration rattles my chest.

"Destroyed," says a mechanical voice through the tiny, muffled speaker.

"Gotcha, Bryan!" Howard yells through the stalks.

"I got him first," Jay counters. "I got the killing shot and you know it."

"Screw you, it was my shot that took him down!" Howard aims his plastic gun at Jay's chest and pulls the trigger. A red light shines onto the pack strapped to Jay as the gun makes another *pew* sound and Jay's pack *bloops*.

"Destroyed."

"Not fair, we're supposed to be on the same team!" Jay says.

"Would you guys cut it out?" Mac approaches from behind and reaches a hand down to pull me up. "You guys beat us again. Why do you have to fight about it?"

"It's my laser tag set. Howard's always a jerk about it." Jay reaches over and yanks the gun from Howard's hand and fires off lasers from both guns at Howard's chest pack.

"Destroyed."

We go back to my house and hoover up the leftover diner food from my fridge.

"Dude, you're so lucky you get to eat this all the time," Howard says through a mouthful of chicken tenders.

Jay pokes at a cold, starchy French fry. "I don't know. Leftover fries are disgusting."

Howard reaches over and grabs the fry from Jay's hand.

"Hey, fartknocker!" Jay complains. He picks up the last chicken tender and throws it. It bounces off Howard's forehead.

"Cut it out, guys," Mac says, then rolls his eyes at me.

"It's alright. My mom brings home diner food every day, so it's not that special. At least the pie is still good."

"I bet she scrapes this food off of plates that people don't finish," Jay says. "Probably covered in spit and sneezes."

Howard shrugs off the comments as he picks up the chicken tender that landed on his lap and shoves it in his mouth. "Whatever, more for me."

I lean back and look around. It's good to have the

guys here, even if they can be chaotic at times. When Mom works late, I'm usually just stuck here alone, dreading the passing of each moment, each inch the sun travels west as it disappears.

"It's getting dark," Mac says as he gets to his feet. He chugs the last of his store-brand root beer and crushes the can in his hand. "We better get going soon so we're not biking home in pitch black."

Howard burps and stands up. "Yeah, my parents are going to be pissed if I'm out past nine."

"You're a bunch of babies," Jay says. "Though my sister won't forgive me if I don't get home and watch at least some of *TGIF* with her."

My heart drops as my friends head toward the front door, but I don't say anything. Mac seems to sense my fears as he stops and turns toward me.

"What's up?" he asks.

I fake a smile and shake my head. "It's nothing. Ride safe, dude." Mac does a double take and then shrugs it off. He knows what I'm afraid of but he doesn't believe it. How could I expect him to?

Once they take off on their bikes and ride out of sight, I turn back to the mess on the dining table and the bottomless stack of dishes and pots in the kitchen sink. I don't feel like going to bed yet, so I may as well try to make a dent in the chores so Mom doesn't come home to this dump.

After two hours, things look pretty good around the kitchen, but my eyes grow heavy. Part of me wants to plop down on the couch, pull up the brown and orange knitted afghan blanket, and fall asleep to the TV, but at this hour it's just news or infomercials on every channel and I have no interest in either. Besides, they'll find me down here just as easily as in my room. I've tried it before. I've even hidden in the closet under the stairs. They took me anyway.

I don't bother turning the light on in my room. It'll just make it harder to see what's outside in the dark if it's too bright in here. I look out at the moon, which is dimmed behind a covering of clouds. I watch as the clouds travel across the night sky. Some are a muddled white, but one darker cloud moves among them. For a moment I swear to myself that it's moving faster than the plodding cadence of the others. Weaving off course. Descending ever so slightly as it approaches.

I pull down the shade and jump to my bed. I curl up and pull the comforter over my head. It stinks like my gym shirt and has a greasy feel through the pilling fabric. I can't remember the last time I washed it. Mom stopped caring about things like that years ago, especially after Dad's incarceration.

I lay there, heat from my body and stink from my breath making it uncomfortable, but still better than the alternative. I feel like a toddler under here. *If I can't see them, they can't see me.* I hope. I wish.

Soon the darkness under the covers mutates to the darkness under my eyelids as sleep overtakes me.

I don't know if I dream. I can almost never remember my dreams. I just know it's dark.

Until it isn't.

The light is blinding through my eyelids. Through the covers. I don't even need to open my eyes or pop my head out of the blankets to see their shapes. I can see them in my mind's eye. Those silhouettes. Human-like but not quite right.

Even if I want to move, I can't. Not when they've taken control. There is no fighting back. No protesting. No screaming. My heart speeds up like a race car. My breathing matches it, then breaks and stutters as if I'm bawling uncontrollably like a baby. Something fills my throat and my nostrils, yet I breathe through it all. I want to open my eyes now, but I also don't. And it's cold. So, so cold all around me, and whatever is entering me is frigid. Like icicles piercing into me.

And then I hear a scream. At first, I think it's my own, sounding distant as my soul leaves my body, but I know it's not me. A feeling of recognition washes over me like déjà vu but I can't quite place it. I quickly forget it as a sharp pain stabs into my belly button and I fall into unconsciousness.

A creaking.

I feel as if I'm falling through the air as my eyes open.

I sit up and take in my surroundings in the morning light. The sun shines onto me, its warmth cutting through the crisp dawn air. I'm on the swinging bench on my front porch. The layer of dirt that covered it is caked to my cheeks now. I wipe it off along with the pool of drool and tears that muddied up the dust in the first place. I grab the chains on either side and put my feet down to stop the back-and-forth motion of the bench. I look around and see Mom's car approaching up the road to our farm. She must have worked a double shift again, leaving me alone all night.

No, not alone.

Vulnerable, yes. But never, ever alone.

Chapter Four
MAC

Mac swerved down the street, his bike off-balanced by the bags hanging from either side of his handlebars. On the right, a half-dozen donuts filled a pink box, the corners poking through the plastic grocery bag. On the left, a gallon of milk weighed down another grocery bag. Mac's parents had sent him out to pick up breakfast for the family.

As he turned off First Street toward his neighborhood, Mac passed the grove of trees that encircled much of the town. Housing developments had been built up in neighborhoods that sat at a distance from the center of town, with stretches of forest clustering in any undeveloped portion, and farms like Bryan's out beyond that. Mac sometimes felt it gave the town a claustrophobic feel with trees closing in all around him in some parts, yet at the same time everything was spread out and distant, stretched like putty. Early on a

Saturday morning, the road back into his neighborhood was quiet and empty.

Mac liked the abandoned feel. He could ride in the middle of the street without fear of cars. He liked to pretend he was Charlton Heston's character at the beginning of *The Omega Man*, the last man alive in a big city, free to roam into any building he pleases.

His illusion broke at the sight of a silhouette in the trees. In his shock, he pulled at the brakes on his handles and skidded to a stop.

He first thought it was an animal walking on four legs, but realized it was too tall and not on four legs at all. It was on two feet, only hunched. Staggering in a crooked gait. And then his eyes focused as the shape stepped out of the trees and vomited all over the side of the road.

Jason Unger's hands were on his bare knees as he bent over and heaved out the contents of his stomach. After another couple retches and groans of misery, the boy realized he was being watched. He looked up and met Mac's eyes. Mac flinched and stepped backward, forgetting he was still straddled over his bike. He fell to the pavement, his bike collapsing over him. The plastic milk carton thudded on top of the pink box, likely crushing the donuts into a mess of greasy dough and sprinkles.

Jason took a step into the street and Mac got a better look at him. He wore a white undershirt that had been yellowed from sweat and browned with dirt. He had no pants on, his privates covered only by a pair of boxers. One knee was scraped up, the other bleeding. Crimson dripped down the calf on that side. His hair was mussed. His face wavered between sick, terrified, and angry.

"What the hell are you staring at, Alden? I'll crush you if you don't get out of here!" Jason took another step, but his bare foot met a jagged piece of gravel and he yelped in pain.

"Jason, what happened? Are you okay?"

"I said get out of here!" Jason screamed, and Mac didn't need to be told a third time. He picked up his bike, adjusted the grocery bags, and sped off toward his neighborhood without a glance back.

"He was probably off on an alcohol bender," Jay said through a mouthful of cheese pizza. He'd brought an extra large over to Mac's house that afternoon to share with the guys.

"Listen to this guy," Howard quipped. "An alcohol bender? Like Jason could even get his hands on a beer."

"My dad said Mr. Unger is a big drinker. Probably has bottles all over their house. My dad even sent Mr. Unger home from work once because he showed up with the smell of beer on his breath. I could use a nice light beer myself right now to wash down this pizza."

"Dude, you'd puke at the taste of it," Mac said.

"Don't you remember what happened last Independence Day? For real, though, I don't think that was it. Jason wasn't drunk, he was terrified of something."

"Maybe Mr. Unger dropped Jason off on the far side of the woods, gave him a thirty second head start, and then went in after him to beat him up if he caught him."

"Enough with theories about Jason's dad, Jay," Howard said. He reached for the final slice in the box.

Jay ignored him and went on. "He has PTSD from Vietnam. My dad says sometimes he sees Mr. Unger yelling at himself in the car before he comes into the office for work."

"Speaking of PTSD," Howard said, "where the hell is Bryan? He knew we were meeting up at one o' clock."

"Don't be a dick." Mac reached across the table and pulled the slice out of Howard's hands. "Save that one for Bryan. We should have saved two. He'll be here soon."

The side door in the kitchen opened and two girls walked in. Larissa was Mac's sister, one year his senior. Like Mac, she had dark blonde hair and stood about five foot six. She was considered tall for a girl while Mac had gotten teased for being one of the shorter boys in the class. Fortunately, he had Jay to make him look tall when they stood next to each other. People often mistook Larissa and Mac for twins, something they both hated. It was about all they could ever agree on.

Jay and Howard both stood at the sight of her. "Oh, hey Larissa," Jay said in what he apparently considered to be a smooth voice. He pointed to the paper grocery bags she carried in each hand. "Let me give you a hand with those."

Larissa rolled her eyes and dropped her voice to mimic the one Jay had used. "Oh hey, dipshit. I think I can carry this myself the last three feet to the counter."

"Hey Mackie, catch," the other girl called out from behind Larissa. A box spun through the air and hit Mac in the forehead. "Your mom asked us to pick up Shark Bites for you at the grocery store."

Mac looked down at the colorful box of fruit snacks that clattered to the floor. "Um, thanks," he said. He cringed as his voice cracked. He looked up to see Violeta Castro smiling at him. He wasn't sure whether it was a mocking smirk or a legitimate smile. All he knew was that she was gorgeous. Not necessarily what many of the other boys at school would consider *hot*. The town was as white as it gets. Everyone not two or three shades away from albino was unofficially delegated to *other* status by most of the in-crowd. Mac was happy to not be part of that crowd. He wouldn't have picked a different group of friends if given a chance. Neither, apparently, would his sister, who had stuck with Violeta through middle school and more than two years of high school so far. They were as close of friends as Mac and his buddies. He quickly looked away as he felt the heat burning through his cheeks. He picked up the box and realized it had been torn open on one corner. He looked back to Violeta at the sound of a package crinkling.

"I took a pack for myself on the walk home," Violeta said, holding up the wrapper. "Hope you don't mind."

"The white ones are my favorite," Howard said. "I don't even know what flavor it is."

"Mystery flavor," Jay said.

"White cherry, I think," Larissa said.

"Damn good is what it is." Violeta walked over to the table and reached into the box that Mac still held. "I'll have another one, thank you very much."

"Hey, you ordered pizza without me, butt-breath?" Larissa asked. She reached over the table and grabbed the last slice from the box.

"Wait, we're saving that slice for Bryan!"

"I don't see that sad-boy loser anywhere." Larissa tore the piece in half and gave the part with the crust to Violeta.

"That's what we call him too," Jay said, giving Howard a high five. "Boo-yeah!"

Mac got up and stomped out of the kitchen. There was a phone in the kitchen but he needed to get away from the others. He passed through the living room and into the den. This was the one room his parents allowed to get messy. The desk was piled with stacks of bills and junk mail that surrounded the keyboard and monitor. The trackball was buried somewhere under the mess. A fan whirred loudly inside the tower of the computer Mac's dad called a *386*, whatever that meant. Mac plopped into the desk chair and reached over the stacks for the phone. He dialed Bryan's number from memory.

"Hello?" a woman said from the other side of the line.

"Hi, Mrs. Adams. It's Mac. Can I please speak with Bryan."

"Well, Mackenzie, I'm not sure if Leslie wants to talk. He's locked himself in his room all day. I went to bed this morning after work and never once heard him leave his room. Do you think something is wrong with him?"

"Just some jerk at school giving him a hard time," Mac said, but he knew it was more than Jason's antics that bothered him. "Could you tell him I called?"

"I'll try. I leave for the night shift at seven tonight, so I should see him by then. Say hello to your mother for me," she replied and hung up the phone.

Mac put the receiver back in its cradle and sat there, gazing into the powered-off computer monitor. His mind went to Jason Unger of all people. He despised the brute as much as anyone, but having seen Jason's disheveled state that morning, something unsettled him. The look of fright and utter despair in Jason's eyes before he noticed Mac's presence. The way he had stumbled out of the woods on the opposite side of town from his house, wearing nothing but what he'd apparently gone to bed in the night before.

And then there was Bryan and whatever he was dealing with. The alleged night visits. The warped figures that Bryan claimed surrounded him as he lay helpless. Bryan had described them as looking stretched out. Features jumbled and unclear. Like what reflected in the monitor just in front of Mac right now.

Mac jumped out of his chair as the stretched-out figure approached him. He turned around at the sound of the footsteps.

"Hey Mac, sorry. I didn't mean to sneak up on you like that." Violeta stopped in the doorway of the den with her hands up in a placating gesture. "Everything okay?"

"I just wasn't expecting anyone to walk in here right then. Um, what's up?"

"Your sister stormed off to her room," Violeta said with a raised eyebrow and a smirk that showed this was something that happened often.

"Let me guess. Jay?"

"That little dude really has a thing for her. Larissa said you need to get them out of the house before she loses it and shanks him with a kitchen knife." She stepped back out of the doorway so Mac could gather his friends. "Specifically a butter knife so that the dismemberment takes longer than a steak knife."

"Alright, I'll get them out of her hair."

Mac walked out of the den but stopped as Violeta's fingers wrapped around his left wrist. He turned to her, shocked by her touch.

"Is something bothering you? Just because I'm your sister's friend, doesn't mean we can't be friends too."

"Just worried about Bryan. He's going through a hard time with his dad and everything. We're going to go find a way to cheer him up. Have fun with the ice queen." Mac gave her an embarrassed smile and ran off to the kitchen before his friends started World War Three with his sister.

"Where are we going?" Howard asked from his bike a few feet behind Mac.

They were on the road out of Mac's neighborhood, though there were significantly more cars in the afternoon. The boys stuck to the edge of the paved shoulder.

"I'll know when I see it," Mac called back. From the side of the road, he was certain they would come across a dried-up puddle of puke at any moment. "Here!" he called. He hit his brakes without warning, causing Howard to swerve. His bike hit Jay's, and the shorter boy veered off into the road. A passing driver pounded down on her horn as the car jumped the yellow center lines to avoid running over the teens.

"You almost killed me!" Jay yelled. He jumped off his bike and pushed it at Howard, who stumbled back in his attempt to dodge it. The pair screamed at each other in the background as Mac engaged his kickstand and left the bike just off the shoulder of the road.

"Guys, come on," Mac uttered as he stepped into the tree line. A few feet in, he could still hear Howard and Jay bickering at each other. "Guys!"

"Where are you going?" Jay asked. "There must be ticks...or *bears* in there."

"There are no bears around here, moron," Howard said. "But Mac, I don't think we should go in there."

"It's just the woods, guys. We used to play in here when we were kids." Mac stepped deeper into the grove of trees. It was true that they had spent a lot of time among these trunks and branches as children. They'd even found an abandoned treehouse that, as far as they knew, hadn't belonged to anybody as it was on public land. But as they grew older and their interests shifted into video games and girls, they had lost a bit of their wonder. Their sense of adventure. It had been perhaps four years since they last explored these woods.

He looked around for any sign that Jason had passed through here, be it trampled flowers or broken branches, but it was a foolish endeavor. Mac was no tracker.

"I'm telling you, we're going to find a bunch of discarded bottles. Probably seniors having a party here last night and Jason Unger just crashed it and pilfered all their drinks," Jay said.

"I think I have to agree with that theory," Howard seconded. Mac ignored them and moved on.

After a few minutes, Mac stopped. He lifted a hand to quiet his friends, who were arguing over whether Lisa, Jessie, or Kelly from *Saved By the Bell* would make the best girlfriend. They cut off their heated debate to see what had their friend so worked up. After a moment, Howard spoke.

"I don't hear anything."

"Exactly," Mac said. "No road noise. We're far from the street now and still no sign of a party. Do you think they'd have a kegger this deep into the woods?"

"Maybe not, but somebody's been here recently," Jay said. Mac followed his gaze to their right.

"What the hell is that?" Mac asked. He jogged twenty feet in that direction into what turned out to be a very new clearing. At least a dozen trees had fallen, though it didn't appear to have been done by a professional. Rather than the clean cuts of a chainsaw, these stumps stood jagged out of the ground, surrounded by the rest of the trunks sprawled out around them haphazardly. Several of the downed trees appeared scorched, covered in a charred black film.

"Maybe he was sleepwalking?" Jay asked.

Howard slapped Jay's right shoulder. "With a pack of matches and a can of gasoline? And he tried to burn down the town because of a bad dream? Get real."

"I don't know, man. How would you explain this, Mac?"

Mac turned. His friends expected an answer from him. He wasn't the smartest or bravest among them, but they always said he kept a level head. The problem was, he found confidence in Bryan's presence, and Bryan wasn't here now. He looked away from them, unsure what to say to appease their curiosity. He walked into the carnage, careful not to tear up his legs on the splintered wood. He got to what he thought was the center and stepped up onto one of the fallen trunks. He looked around.

"Whatever it is," Mac said, "it's almost a perfect circle."

Howard shook his head. "There's no way Jason made this. The dude can barely write his own name."

"Then what are we looking at? What the hell did this?"

Chapter Five
BRYAN

With Mom gone, I take to the porch. I have no idea how I ended up on the bench swing this morning, yet I don't feel fear about this spot. As if the bench is a safe space for me. I push off lightly with my feet and let the bench rock. The overhang groans as the chains pull down and I swing back and forth. The motion soothes me and soon I don't even notice the groaning and creaking. My eyelids grow heavy and sleep overtakes me.

The dreams come quickly but I forget them almost as soon as they happen. Yet elements of them stick with me; they are so vivid. Emerging from darkness. A filthy, rough tarp. Low metal walls. The smell of rust and exhaust. Bumps and sudden swerves. Dirt flying up all around. I'm not alone. Maybe two adults near me sitting up, looking concerned. I feel a mass at my side but can't turn to see what or who it is. The adults point at something. We're being pursued. A bright light flashes, blinding me. Screams all around. Then darkness all over again.

Ding ding

I startle back into consciousness on the porch swing as Mac, Jay, and Howard ride up on their bikes, Jay thumbing the bell on his right handlebar. I stand to greet them and the bench swings back and hits me behind the knees, sending me stumbling a couple steps in my sleepy stupor.

"What are you guys doing here?" I ask through a yawn.

Mac gets off his bike and leans it against the porch. "You couldn't come to us, so we came to you."

"No pizza, though," Jay says. "You missed out on that."

Howard heaves a backpack from the walkway, and it lands with a *thud* on the porch. I look at the other guys and notice they all have bulging packs and sleeping bags that they hauled all the way out here.

"What's with the bags?" I ask.

"If you ask my mom, I'm sleeping at Mac's tonight," Howard says.

Jay drops his next to Howard's. "Same."

"And I'm at Jay's house," Mac says.

I smile at this. "I've never seen you lie successfully to your parents, Mac."

"My parents are shopping at the mall in Raventree Hollow, so I just left a note. Easy."

"Unless your sister rats you out," Jay jests.

"Wouldn't surprise me if Violeta followed you. Looked like you two were in love this afternoon," Howard says. He makes smooching sounds and I see Mac's cheeks go red immediately. We all crack up at this.

"Shut up, guys," Mac says. He looks me in the eyes. "Whatever you're going through, we want to be here for you. I know your mom is working another night shift, so we thought we'd stay the night here and keep you company."

"I'm not a toddler. I don't need babysitters." I turn to walk into the house, wanting to slam the door, but as I pull the screen door open and glance at the stairs leading up to the dim second floor, I pause and turn back. With a deep breath, I release the frustration. I've at least gotten that much out of all the shrinks I've seen. "But I'm glad to have my brothers here. Come on in, guys."

There isn't much to offer them from the kitchen. They already ate up the leftovers last night and Mom didn't bring anything home today. Still, Jay susses out a frozen pizza from the back of the freezer and we split it among the four of us while playing board games at the kitchen table. The dim dusk sky outside casts an eeriness over the house, but the laughter from my friends brightens up the place and I already feel better about everything. Before I know it, the sun is gone completely, but we continue with the games and laughter for a while longer with no adults here to tell us to quiet down.

"Should we sleep in the barn like old times?" Howard asks as yawns overtake us. I look at the clock on the stove to find it's nearly ten.

"I haven't cleaned in there for months, but we can bring the broom out," I say.

While the guys brush their teeth and get ready for sleep, I run across the yard into the sagging barn behind my house. I don't know how the barn still stands, or how it even keeps the rainwater out with how misshapen it is, but it's been here longer than my parents have been alive and I hope it still stands when I have kids of my own one day. This is where we had sleepovers when we were younger, Howard and Mac and me. Jay hadn't moved to town yet, and it was long before my dad's arrest and everyone's parents finding out about how much of a piece of shit Dad was. They still knowingly allowed their kids to come play at my place in those days, and we'd have the best time out in the barn. We felt like kings here without our parents to tell us it was time for lights out or to quiet down. We'd eat junk food and drink soda all night long and play with our action figures and wrestle and curse. Those were the best days.

The barn door opens and the guys come up the stairs just as I finish sweeping up the loft. I don't tell them about the spiders I brushed out of the rafters. If there's one thing that'll break Jay out of his cool-guy act, it's spiders. That boy will scream in a pitch I thought was reserved for opera singers when he sees a common house spider, never mind the black widows that call the dark corners of this barn home.

"Bro, you can come clean up at my house tomorrow morning," Howard jokes. "Sunday is when my parents make me do all the floors."

"This is so clean, you could eat off it." Jay lays out his old *Ninja Turtles* sleeping bag on the floor of the loft. It's the size of sleeping bag the rest of us had outgrown years ago, but not Jay. My old one was a *He-Man* one. That might catch me some weird looks if I still tried to use it these days. Mac had a *Ghostbusters* sleeping bag when we were younger, and Howard's was *G.I. Joe*. I'd be lying if I said I don't kind of miss those. Now all we have are boring navy blue or burgundy camping bags from Montgomery Ward. Not quite the same.

At least one thing hasn't changed. We still have this space to use for sleepovers, even if it's been a while since the last one. Dad had laid out a partial roll of linoleum flooring left over from one of the side-jobs he did during the winter season. I was seven or eight at the time and thought it was my very own apartment like the one the Fonz had over Richie Cunningham's garage in the *Happy Days* reruns. Mom told me later that she had convinced him to do it in hopes I could escape his wrath. She tried sending me out there a few times when he was in his moods, but it didn't help. He chased me down and it was only worse.

"I need to get my bedding from the house," I say as I lean the broom against the wall and head down the steps. The outside air hits me like a frigid slap in the face. I don't remember even being the slightest bit chilly twenty minutes ago when I had entered the barn. Nor as dark. The porch light was off, and the guys must have shut off all the lights inside the house on their way out. The sudden drop in temperature feels like a sign to me. It's going to be another bad night, I'm sure of it. I take a deep breath and run.

Within ten seconds, I'm up the porch steps and into the house. I pause as I step into the foyer. I hear a *thud* from the back of the house, and then silence. A rat? Something the guys pushed to the edge of a shelf by accident that toppled over? I glance down at my watch. It's too early for *them* to be here. Isn't it? I dart up the stairs, taking them two at a time, and don't stop until I'm in the bathroom. The only interior doors with locks are this bathroom and the one downstairs. I flip the lock and find my breath.

Thud!

Downstairs still, but it's moved to another room, perhaps the kitchen. Something higher pitched follows it. My first thought is laughter, but it doesn't sound like my friends. Some kind of language used by *them*? I can't remember ever hearing them speak or communicate to each other like that, but that doesn't mean it never happened in my presence. Even in the times when I felt like I was awake, it was all so hazy, the way a dream feels. Many of the details dissipated by morning, so perhaps I forgot about their sounds.

It's then that I feel the loneliness of the house, knowing my friends are just across the yard in the barn. This place is cold. Dark. Despite the walls and the locked bathroom door, I somehow feel more exposed here without my friends nearby. I have to go back out there, to the safety in numbers. I leave my toothbrush untouched and reach for the doorknob. Any other time, the click of the lock wouldn't even register in my ears, but with intruders in the house, I can't help but feel it's like a gunshot firing. Surely they heard it downstairs.

A deep breath. Turn the handle. Run.

It's not as easy to skip steps going down, but I attempt it anyway. Four steps down, I realize it's a bad idea. My heel brushes the edge of the sixth step as I overshoot, and I come down too hard on the seventh. I roll the rest of the way down and lay sprawled out on the first-floor landing. Stars scatter across my vision before they narrow into a singular source.

A light.

I failed. They found me.

"Oh my god, are you okay?"

"Get the light out of his eyes!"

The source of light moves. I blink away the remnants of the brightness. I try to focus on the silhouettes around me. Something's not right. They look too normal to be my intruders. And they certainly don't sound like otherworldly beings. One's face is just like Mac's, but something isn't right about it.

"Larissa?" I groan. "What are you doing here?"

Larissa points to her best friend. "Violeta tricked me into coming out here. She wants to see my idiot brother."

Violeta backhands Larissa on her upper arm. "It's not like there's anything better to do in this town." She reaches down for my right hand and pulls me up to my feet. I stumble back a step but don't feel any shooting pain.

"I think my ankle is okay."

"It was her idea to sneak in the back door," Larissa says.

"Just a prank. I didn't think we'd almost kill him."

I play it off. "No worries. The guys are waiting for me, so I was hurrying back to them. Just lost my balance on the way down."

They glance at each other and don't push it further. They don't look convinced, but like a lot of people, they walk on eggshells around me most of the time after everything with my dad. I sometimes wonder if people think I'm going to turn out to be a violent, abusive creep. Like father, like son. Or, they think I'm going to have an emotional breakdown and cry and they'd be stuck comforting me. Everyone, that is, but Jason Unger. He tries his best every day to push me one direction or the other in hopes that I'll snap. I'll never give him the satisfaction.

With the two girls behind me, I trek out to the barn empty-handed.

"Dude, what the hell?" Mac shouts almost as soon as I open the door to the barn.

"Fancy seeing you ladies here," Jay says from behind the banister of the upstairs loft. I don't know where the robe he wears even came from; maybe it was tucked inside his sleeping bag. It looks like a red velvet smoking jacket, and it hangs open to reveal his skinny bare chest, ribs practically protruding through his skin. Below the waist, he has a pair of boxers on. They're silky red with gold stars. "Larissa, I'm afraid you've caught me in the middle of my bedtime routine."

Howard leaps up from behind and slams his pillow hard into the side of Jay's head, sending the smaller boy plummeting to his sleeping bag. "Got you!"

"How uncivilized," Jay says. I laugh as he spots his own *Ninja Turtles* sleeping bag and rushes to turn it upside down so only the plain green fabric is visible before the girls climb the stairs and spot the childish object. From where Larissa, Violeta, and I stand downstairs, we can't see the print but I know what he's doing. I turn to the girls. Larissa makes a show of rolling her eyes, but I'm surprised to see her make a second glance upstairs. Not at Jay, nor at her seething brother, but at Howard. My eyes shoot up to him and I swear I see something pass between them for a very prolonged second.

I notice Violeta's gaze follows the same path mine

takes, from Larissa's eyes to Howard's, just before both look away from each other as if to hide something.

"Whatever," Larissa says, turning to Violeta. "I've seen enough to make me sick for a week. Did you get whatever you came for?"

"Play it cool, girl. I just wanted to see what it is these little shits do together here." Violeta pushes past her annoyed friend and ascends the stairs. She waves up to Mac at the top landing. "Hey, Mackenzie. No birthday suit for you like Hugh Hefner here?" she asks, gesturing toward Jay. I can tell Jay has momentarily lost whatever burst of confidence he had a minute ago as he digs himself into his sleeping bag.

Mac rolls his eyes just like his sister, but his lips quiver into a hint of a smile. "I wait until the guys fall asleep and then I take it all off," he jokes. I must admit, I'm proud of him. He's usually so nervous around girls.

"Freaking gross!" Larissa gags next to me. She turns and storms out of the barn, slamming the big door behind her. The entire barn rattles as if it's going to collapse.

"What a strong lady," Jay says from his sleeping bag. Howard slips on his shoes and runs down the stairs just as I start to make my way up.

"Where are you off to?" I ask him.

"Bathroom," Howard says briskly and disappears into the night. I shrug it off and make my way up the stairs where Violeta has already plopped down on Mac's sleeping bag and pillow while Mac and Jay watch with confusion.

"Seriously, what are you doing here?" Mac asks her. Since I forgot my own bedding, I sit down on Howard's bunched up sleeping bag.

"Just testing a theory," Violeta says.

"Proving it, more like," I add, knowing exactly what she's talking about. I have no idea how or when it could have happened, but somehow Mac's sister and Howard have become secret lovers. I search Mac's face, but I don't see any sign of realization. He's lost in Violeta's presence. Sweat forms on his forehead despite the evening chill.

Jay stands up and pulls his robe tight around himself. "I think I'll go check on Larissa," he says. There's a slight edge to his voice as if he's just coming to the same understanding as the rest of us. The last thing we need is another reason for Howard and Jay to get at each other's throats.

I reach up and grab his robe. "Just sit back down and relax, dude." He glares at me, but my grip remains tight and he finally gives up and returns to his bedding.

Across from me, Violeta looks over to Mac and pats the remainder of his sleeping bag. "Come on and relax," she says. To my surprise, Mac goes over and sits next to her. She scoots closer, filling in the gap he's left, and punches his bent knee playfully.

We sit around and gossip and joke for what must be

half an hour before Howard returns and tells Violeta that Larissa is ready to go home. "Well, it was fun, boys," Violeta says. She looks at Mac for a moment, and that's all it takes for his cheeks to flush.

"I, um, well, g-g-goodnight," he stutters and looks away from her. Violeta rises to her feet, bemusement on her face.

"Smooth," Jay says, then slams his head back down onto his pillow. I stand and give Howard his sleeping bag back and walk Violeta down the stairs to the door.

"Drive safe," I say as she passes through the barn doorway. I stand there while she walks up the path to her car. She fades into the darkness, but I remain at the open barn door. A slight whirring sound catches my ear. Not a car, as a few seconds later I see her interior dome light come on as Violeta opens the door of her ride, Larissa waiting impatiently in the passenger seat. The engine starts and sounds nothing like what I thought I heard. I pull the barn door closed and rush up the stairs where the guys are already lying down.

They pretend to be asleep, but I can feel the tension in the air. Jay feels betrayed by Howard over Larissa, whom Jay has been in love with for the last two years. Mac is also pissed about Howard's apparent relationship with his sister. Howard probably feels the invisible daggers from both of them and resents them for it.

Despite it all, though, I'm just glad these guys are here. With them around, perhaps I'll sleep well tonight, undisturbed by any unwanted visitors. Surely with three witnesses around, I won't be bothered.

Right?

And yet...

Chapter Six

BRYAN

The light hits different than it would in my room, combed through the boards of the barn. The entire structure groans under the pressure as the light reaches for me. I had settled into a pile of clothes and jackets in between Mac and Howard and fell asleep immediately, but now as I lay in the path of the blinding white beam, the pieces of makeshift bedding pop away from me like wayward popcorn.

In my periphery, I see Mac stir slightly. *Wake up*, I think. I want to scream it. *Wake up!* No voice escapes my throat despite my frantic efforts. The more I try, the more I struggle to breathe. I hear my labored panting as if at a distance, as if I'm outside of my own body. Mac is within reach if I can only move my arm. Any other time, I don't even need to think about which muscles to engage for common movements, but right now I can't even force a single finger to budge.

Please, Mac. Howard. Jay. Please!

They don't wake up.

The shutters rattle, then fly open. I expect loose debris from around the barn to fly over me and get sucked through the opening like dust into a vacuum, but the only thing that moves is my own body. I'm lifted into the air. I see myself approaching the window and for a moment all I can think is that I'm going to slam into the frame, but the light guides me out untouched. I'm two stories up in the air over my yard for just a moment, wishing the light would break and send me plummeting to my death below so I can just end all of this.

The light grows more intense, yet I don't feel heat. I don't even feel cold. I just feel stasis. Forced on me. Unwelcome. Brighter. Brighter. And then...

Darkness.

Chapter Seven
BRYAN

Darkness.

Chapter Eight
BRYAN

Darkness. But then...

A flash of light.

Haze. No smell of smoke, though. More like fog. Or maybe like dry ice. It has a color. A slight, pink-tinted light. It hangs in the air like a vapor cloud, illuminating the room around me.

A shadowy figure cuts through it, but I can't make out who or what it belongs to. It's as if the pink fog is purposely hiding it, obscuring it like the witnesses getting interviewed on those cop shows, their identity hidden for their own protection. The fog twists, wraps around the figure, guarding the being. A shadowed arm stretches toward me. Something in its grasp. A sharp pain in my belly, and my vision fades into darkness once more.

Just before I slip back into unconsciousness, a deep scream rings out. There's something so familiar about it, about who is making that frantic sound. In the moment, I recall hearing it during other nights like this. What I can't dredge up in my memory is who that scream is coming out of.

And then I'm gone.

Chapter Nine
BRYAN

Rays of the night's full moon poke like needles through the rough tarp draped over my head. I try to sit up and throw it off me, but with each attempt, I'm hampered. Pushed back down. Pinned against the bed of the truck on which I lay. I realize the struggle is pointless, so I give up and cry. The guys aren't here to see this anyways so fuck it. Tears and snot stream down my cheeks.

"Shit," a gruff voice says. "I think it's coming after us." I try to place the voice. It seems to belong to a woman who sounds as if she's smoked a pack of cigarettes for each meal every day for decades. Like carpenter nails scratching around inside a coffee tin. "Speed us the hell up for Christ's sake!" I hate to think what she sounds like happy, but right now her voice is full of panic.

"Just keep the boy down and stay calm," a man says

in a deep, mumbling tone, but even he sounds uneasy. I want to scream at them, tell them to let me out of this tarp, but something feels strange in my mouth, like my tongue is numb. Like I've been to the dentist to have teeth pulled, when they give me that gas. So I lay there and continue listening for signs of what is happening and who these people are.

It's a pickup truck, I've no doubt about that. With every bump in the road, I hear debris clanking around me in the bed, but also a squeaking somewhere in the undercarriage. The suspension, maybe? That sound gives me a picture of a dumpy, rusted old truck filled with dumpy old folks. Three of them at least if there are two here to pin me down and another driving. And these roads, seemingly cratered with huge potholes and littered with bumps that cause me to slam my head each time we drive over one, not to mention making the suspension squeal like an abused pig.

"They're gaining on us!" the man yells this time, sounding more paranoid than the woman.

"Almost out of it now," the driver calls back. This one a man with a somewhat smoother voice than the other two, maybe a little younger than his companions with less tobacco smoke in his history.

The truck takes a sharp right turn, sending my captors tumbling off their knees and me rolling across the bed twice and slamming into the wall of the truck. For a moment I see only pure darkness before I realize my heavy eyelids are closed from some drug or whatever has been done to me. The wind hitting my face tells me something else though—my head is out of the tarp now. With all my willpower, I force myself to open my eyes, and then I scream. The sound is strange at first until I break through whatever has been hindering me.

That's when I see it. The brightness in the sky is not the moon at all. It is something round. Light emanates from it, but it's nothing that belongs to this world or even this solar system. It's following the truck, though I'm confused why it remains behind us when it could easily outrun us or use whatever contraption it employs to take me from my room at night.

"The boy!" yells the woman, and I turn toward the sound of her voice. Remnants of the cutting light in the sky fill my vision and I lose her in the shadows.

"Taking care of it," the man replies, and I realize that he's right next to my head. "Sorry, kid, but it's for your own good." I see his silhouette for a fraction of a second before he lowers a rag onto my face. I struggle to breathe. A sharp chemical smell fills my nostrils, and then I'm back into darkness. Unconscious. One step from death.

Chapter Ten
MAC

Tires kicked up rocks on the expansive gravel driveway of the Adams farm. Ancient, rusted suspension squealed over the potholes in the unkept road back to town. A boy was pulled out of slumber from the sounds.

Mac sat up and slapped at his left cheek. The early morning sun shined in on him like a spotlight on the floor of the barn loft. It was just enough light to see the spider drop to the dusty floor and skitter away. Mac reached up to rub his flesh and was relieved to find no swelling mound from a bite where he'd felt the spider crawling.

The pulsing bundles of blankets and sleeping bags around him told him his buddies were still asleep. Mac rose to his feet and looked through the windowpanes when confusion dawned on him. He distinctly remembered Bryan opening the window and reaching outside to pull the shutters closed the night before. He recalled the creaking of the rusting hinges, and how Bryan had reached for a little block of wood to help hammer the dilapidated lock into place to hold the shutters together in the event of any wind. Yet, there they were, wide open to let in the sunlight.

Wait, he thought. *Bryan!*

Mac turned back toward the sleepers. Jay under his colorful *Ninja Turtles* bag. Howard in the burgundy. His own empty sleeping bag. Bryan had come back with the girls last night instead of the bedding he'd gone to collect, so the guys all piled their jackets and extra clothing on him to form a makeshift bed before they went to sleep. Those items were scattered about in a path to the window with no trace that Bryan had slept under them.

Mac recalled the sounds of a vehicle outside that had woken him up just a minute ago. He walked closer to the window and scanned the yard. From his perch, he could see the side yard where an herb and vegetable garden had once thrived, feeding not only the Adams family but also anyone who patronized the Adams's stall at the farmers' market in town. Now, it was nothing more than a weed-infested mess. A cracking cement pathway led past it, stretching from the barn to a set of steps up to the wraparound porch of Bryan's house just to the side of the front door. Mac had expected to see Mrs. Adams's car parked in front of the porch, but only the kids' bicycles filled that space.

Who else would have driven here this early? Mac wondered. Movement pulled his eyes back to the porch. On the far side of the front door, Bryan sat up on the gently rocking bench, looking around with confusion. *What the hell is he doing out there?*

"Sad-boy mode already? It's not even seven in the morning."

Mac turned his head to find Howard looking over his shoulder. "Dude, don't even start. Whatever that was about last night between you and my sister, I don't even want to hear anything from you."

Howard grimaced. "Come on, Mac, there's nothing to be upset about."

"Oh yes there is," Jay said as he climbed out of his sleeping bag. "Larissa is mine and you know it."

"What the hell, Jay? She's not anyone's. She's my damn sister!"

"Who can make decisions for herself," Howard said. "I like her, and she likes me. That's all there is to it."

Jay threw his head back as if he'd been punched in the face. "But you know I've been in love with her since the moment I first laid eyes on her. She's my dream woman!"

"And clearly she did not feel the same way." Howard turned back to Mac. "Larissa and I are dating now. None of us losers have had a girlfriend in a while, but now I do. If you can't be happy for me, then maybe we were never really friends to begin with."

"But why my sister? There are a hundred other single girls at school."

"Forget you guys," Howard said. He stormed back to his sleeping bag, tucked his pillow inside the folds, and rolled it all up into a tight bundle. He pulled the attached strings around it and tied the knots, then left the barn without another word. Mac and Jay waited until he slammed the door before running down to the house to catch the inevitable conversation between Howard and Bryan.

Mac couldn't see Howard's face from behind, but he imagined the scowl his angry friend must have displayed because even Bryan looked too afraid to speak. Howard plopped onto his bike and rode off down the driveway without a greeting to Bryan or a goodbye to anyone.

They watched in silence as Howard disappeared down the road toward town before Jay spoke. "Well, this day is starting off pretty rad already."

Part of Mac wanted to laugh at the comment; if anyone knew how to break the tension in an awkward situation, it was Jay. However, something didn't feel right between the remaining boys. Something dark flowed from Bryan in particular. Mac studied his distressed demeanor. "Don't tell me they came for you when we were all around and we didn't even wake up for it."

"I slept like a baby," Jay said. "Heartbreak will do that to me."

Bryan ignored him, his eyes locked on Mac's and full

of misery. "You didn't even budge, Mac. The lights were so bright, and you didn't wake. I tried to yell out to you, but I couldn't. Nothing would come out." His voice shook as if he was on the verge of tears.

"How is that possible?" Mac asked. "We were right next to you. The light should have woken us up, or the window opening. I saw the shutters; they were wide open even though I know we closed them before bed."

"So the dude sleepwalks," Jay said dismissively. "Not much mystery there. A lot of people do it."

Bryan hammered his fist on the bench. "But do they sleepwalk into the back of a stranger's pickup truck and hide under some kind of tarp as a UFO chases after them? Because that's something I can actually remember this morning."

"'Join me for another edition of *Unsolved Mysteries*,'" Jay quipped in a deep voice, imitating host Robert Stack. "Come on, Bry, we've all seen that show. Maybe you've just watched it one too many times."

Bryan stared at him for a moment with a pained expression and then turned around and stormed into the house.

"Not cool, man," Mac said. "You know he's going through a lot of shit. Look, I'll go talk to him. Maybe we should cut this sleepover short and call it a day. I'll see you at school on Monday."

"But Mac, I was only joking. You can't believe that alien garbage he's claiming, can you?"

Mac ignored Jay's protests. He followed Bryan into

the house and closed the door before Jay could tag along. Inside, Mrs. Adams's metallic-tinged voice was projecting through the answering machine's speaker.

"—lawyer's office for a meeting and then I'll grab some groceries, so I won't be home until at least nine. I know we're low on food so just use some bread from the freezer for a peanut butter and jelly sandwich and I'll make you eggs when I get home. Love you." The machine clicked and whirred as the tape stopped and rewound, ready for its next usage.

"I may as well live here by myself," Bryan said. "She's never here anymore. Working all night, errands during the day. I think she has a boyfriend, too."

"Seriously?" Mac asked about the last point. "Go Mrs. A!"

Bryan glared at him, but Mac knew it was more playful than angry. "Is that how you feel about Howard and your sister?"

"That's different," Mac retorted, "unless you mean your mom is dating one of our friends. It certainly isn't me, but Jay has always ranked your mom above the rest of ours."

Bryan picked up a ballpoint pen from the counter next to the phone and threw it at Mac. "Very funny, butt-face. Thanks for sending the guys away. I'm not in the mood for their crap this morning."

Bryan went to the freezer and retrieved four slices of bread from a bag of Wonder Kids. He used a butter knife to scrape off the layer of ice crystals and microwaved the slices before slathering on the crunchy peanut butter. He skipped the jelly after finding a colony of mold spores sprouting inside the jar and threw on some blackening bananas instead. He and Mac sat down and scarfed down the sandwiches in silence.

After their plates were both empty, Mac spoke. "Do you have any idea whose truck it was?"

"No."

"Would you recognize it if you saw it? We could ride around town and try to spot it," Mac suggested.

Bryan seemed to consider this for a minute and then shrugged his shoulders. "It's worth a try. Let's do it."

Chapter Eleven
BRYAN

We ride throughout the morning, stopping for donuts before the church crowd completely obliterates the selection. Mac goes for a maple bar and a blueberry cake donut while I select the last apple fritter and a raised glaze. No hot chocolate since we eat while we ride. Before I take my first bite, I realize I haven't brushed my teeth in a couple days. It's been a rough weekend, so I cut myself some slack and dig into the sugary goodness.

After the fritter, I demolish the other donut. "Great call, Mac," I say through a mouthful. "I'm feeling better about things already." I swallow the last bite as we swoop through a parking lot of the out-of-business drive-thru burger restaurant and toss the grease-spotted donut bags onto the heap of an overflowing trashcan. I scratch at an itch on my scalp and pull my hand away to see a clump of hair stuck to the glaze on my fingers. "What the hell?"

Mac brakes when he notices I've stopped riding. "Something wrong?" he asks as he circles back around toward me. "What's on your hand?"

I wipe the hairs onto my jeans and reach back up. On the right side just above my ear, I grasp a few more hairs. They pull off without resistance.

Mac's jaw drops. "That's... that's not supposed to happen."

"No shit," I mutter as I stare at it. "Did you guys play a prank on me last night? Shave the side of my head or something?"

"We'd never do something like that. It would leave too much evidence. We'd just slowly poison you or something. Wipe your lunch in bird poop when you're not looking, stuff like that."

I glare at him.

"Sorry, not a time for jokes," he says. "Let's go to Jay's house. It's Sunday, so his dad should be home. He'll be able to tell you what's happening."

"Nah, Jay will just make fun of me again." We drop our bikes and sit on the curb of the drive-thru lane. I rub at the spot the hair had come from. It's smooth.

"Dude, you have a little bald spot there now," Mac points out. "Stop scratching at it and maybe nothing else will fall out."

"Why is it doing this?"

"Does baldness run in your family?" Mac asks.

I think about my family tree. "I never met my grandfather on my dad's side so I can't say about him, but my dad's brothers had full heads of hair. Same with my mom's father. She didn't have any brothers."

"And your..." Mac hesitates. "Your dad? I don't think I ever saw him without a hat. Sorry to bring him up."

"Don't worry about it. And no, he wasn't bald either. He..." A memory comes to me. For years I've tried not to think about him, even the good times. I try to block it all out of my mind, but it's never truly gone. "I think I remember something. There was this time when he was at his worst in those last three years before he finally went to prison. He was raging for probably the tenth straight night after he came in from work. He was upset about my mom accidentally bumping his beer off the armrest of his recliner and he cornered my mom against the television set. At first, he just yelled into her ear while she was trapped there, but the more she tried to lean away from him, the more VHS tapes she knocked off the top of the TV. That's when he started slapping her around. He'd use the back of his hand instead of his fist so it didn't bruise as much.

"I was at the table doing my homework when it all started. I got so upset seeing what he was doing to her, I threw down my pencil and darted across the room. I remember taking a couple steps on the rug and leaping up onto the coffee table and then making the jump at him. I don't know what I planned to do when I got there, but I landed on his back and wrapped one arm around his neck. That stupid cowboy hat he always wore fell off. I used my free hand to grab at his head. The clumps of hair came out without resistance, just like this. I didn't rip them out of his scalp; they were already loose. He..."

I trail off and bawl my eyes out. I don't cry around Jay and Howard if I can help it, but Mac is different. He doesn't judge me for it, won't make fun of me. The last thing I need right now is for this memory to come up, but it looks like Mac is right. "Maybe it really does run in the family," I manage through my sobs. "But why is it happening now? I feel like it's related to what's happening to me at night."

Mac scoots closer and rubs my shoulder to console me. "So you think the... you think the aliens are causing it?"

"Aliens?" a mocking voice says.

"Oh no," Mac and I whisper at the same time. Mac pulls his hand away from my shoulder and we both turn around.

"The only aliens around here are Jay and Howard," Jason Unger says. He moves out of the shadows between the dumpsters and steps toward us. "Where are those two shit-faces anyways? Do they know you're getting fresh without them? They might be jealous when they find out." He kicks a smattering of gravel and dirt from the island between the dumpsters and the drive-thru lane. Gritty residue flings straight into my eyes.

"What the hell?" I yell as I shoot to my feet and rub at my eyes.

"Leave us alone, butt-breath," Mac says.

I clear my eyes enough to take another look at Jason. Despite his mocking sneer, I see something else in his face. His eyes are red even though mine are the ones that just took a load of dirt to them. His have bags under them. His cheeks look raw as if he's been wiping away tears of his own.

"Leave you alone so you can fornicate behind this joint?" Jason asks. He steps closer and lunges for Mac's bike.

"Let go of that!" Mac yells and jumps toward him. Jason is faster. He grasps a handle and the frame, picks it up, and takes off running with it. Once he reaches the sidewalk, Jason sets the bike down, throws one leg over it, and rides away.

"Thanks for the ride!" he calls and disappears out of sight.

"We'll get it back," I promise Mac.

We leave the parking lot, Mac walking empty-handed and me walking my bike. We head down Gardenia Street, our eyes scanning every vehicle parked in a driveway or parking lot, every car zooming past us.

"Too many damn pickup trucks in this town," I say. "Maybe this was a stupid idea."

"It's a small enough place. We'll find what you're looking for sooner or later." Mac stops and cocks his head like a dog processing some new information. "You hear that?"

I listen and realize he's not crazy. Willie Nelson plays over some lousy outdoor speakers, reverberating off the shop walls and down the street. The sound brings back memories I'd rather forget. "They're still using the same loudspeakers up on those poles, I guess."

Mac eyes me with confusion.

"The farmers' market. The one my dad used to sell at."

"I haven't been in a couple of years," Mac says. "Let's check it out."

I follow him toward the source of the music. We cut through an alley between the Prime Cuts Butcher Shop (the less said about the smells emanating from that place's trash cans, the better) and the Wellworth's Fine Candies store. On the other side of the alley, we cross Acorn Lane to the park. An oversized gazebo sits in the center, where the market management is set up with a folding table holding their tape deck, a microphone, and stacks of papers about the various vendors. Another table holds a contraption containing black and white marbles with numbers on them and a crank to mix them up until one falls down a little ramp. The bingo game is a big draw for the elderly crowd, and I remember enjoying it with Mac when we were younger. Especially the pie we won one time when our shared card was the first to get five in a row. Sprouting out around the central gazebo are around two dozen stalls, each with folding tables covered in produce, potted plants, and baked goods. Others have crafts from local artists, or boutique clothing items. Many are set up under canopies to block out the sun. On the outer layer of the circle, pickups and box trucks are parked in the grass, backed up for easy access for the vendors to restock their goods as needed.

Mac leads me into the crowd. There are a lot of people, so I lock my bike up on the side of the gazebo. As we walk through the shoppers, I feel eyes on me. I meet the gaze of Frannie Holman, who specializes in strawberries from her fields that neighbor my family's farm. She flashes a look of pity and I quickly avert my eyes. I get similar expressions from other vendors that I grew up seeing here every weekend in my childhood. Like most people in town, they know the things my dad did to me and my mom, and they would probably apologize for not stepping in to put a stop to it sooner. And it's true, they did nothing. My dad would backhand me in front of all of them for running off with Mac, or verbally berate my mom if she miscounted change for a customer, and nobody ever said a word. I don't hate them, though. My dad was a terrifying guy behind his slick smile even then, so I can't blame them for being afraid.

"Let's get out of here, Mac."

He turns to me. "Look at all the trucks, though. Maybe one of these is what we're looking for."

"I don't think so. These trucks get here at dawn.

There's no way one of them would have been cruising around town kidnapping kids and returning them home at that time. They'd have been loading up the trucks since five in the morning to bring their goods to the market."

Mac shoots an arm out to stop me before I barrel into a woman with a stroller that halted just in front of us.

"Back it up, folks, back it up," a man shouts. I recognize his voice as Barry Jules, the guy who has operated the market since before I was born. He was a witness at my dad's trial, describing the abuse he'd seen in this very park over the years.

We join the crowd in backing up as Barry waves to the driver of an idling pickup at the edge of the park. The driver waves back. I see the white lights come on indicating the transmission is in reverse, and the truck hops the curb and backs into the park toward the empty space between Maggie Fielder's antique stand and Henry O'Marley's table of fresh baked sweet breads.

The tires bounce as they meet the sidewalk. A high-pitched sound comes from under the truck and I cock my head. As the pickup backs over the little rises and dips in the grass field, the suspension sings like a mule in pain. I know this noise. I've heard it before. As recently as this morning.

"Dude, you okay?" Mac asks. I shake out of my

stupor and notice my jaw has dropped low. I close my mouth and turn toward him.

"Let's go sit for a minute," I say, gesturing toward a bench that has just been vacated by a mom and her twin toddlers. We walk over and brush crumbs off from the croissants the kids had eaten there moments earlier.

"That's the one?" Mac points his chin at the truck as it halts and the engine is cut.

"Maybe," I say, not wanting to commit yet. "Let's just watch." The doors open on both sides of the cab. One man exits on the driver's side and a woman and second man slide out from the passenger side. They look old and disheveled, maybe in their mid-to-late sixties, all three with wild white hair like some Grateful Dead rejects. One man has a beard down to his belly like a white-trash Santa Claus, and the other has a biker's handlebar mustache and about a week's worth of stubble. The bearded one wears a thick plaid shirt of faded red and black. The other man has a leather vest over a stained white Van Halen T-shirt. The woman's scraggly mullet isn't too out of the ordinary in this town, and she has a flannel that almost matches the one worn by her husband. I recognize them.

"The Valisellis? Those inbred freaks are who we're looking for?" Mac asks. I say nothing, just watch them as they pop up their canvas overhang, unfold a table, and set out their wares to display. They sport brown leather gloves as they handle their products, which are all made of aluminum soda pop cans, old soup or bean tins, and other sliced and reshaped metal goods. Twirling windmills, airplanes hanging from strings from the canopy frame, cola can flowerpots with root beer flowers sprouting out. A little pig crafted from a chicken noodle soup can and carefully shaped pieces of ginger ale cans.

"I loved those things when I was little," I mutter. I watch them put the last of their items out, interact with passersby and interested patrons. "They were here every weekend just like my family."

"They're weird, but I wouldn't have thought they were *catch-and-release kids* weird," Mac says. "You're sure about this?"

"I'm trying to remember the voices I heard from under that prickly tarp in the back of the truck. It's not clear to me but I do recall a panic in their voices that I don't hear now," I say as I listen to them chat with neighboring vendors and potential customers. "But otherwise they might be the same voices. I can't say for sure."

"Oh my god," a girl says behind us. Mac and I turn to face Larissa. "Mom is flipping out at home and you're just here with your little boyfriend holding hands like an old married couple. This is too good."

"What the hell, Larissa?" Mac asks. He stands up and crosses his arms. "What is Mom upset about?"

Her smile is devious. "Well, this morning she was all upset she didn't have her carrots and celery to make her breakfast smoothie even though she sent me to the supermarket yesterday. Seems I forgot the back side of the shopping list. She was so angry at me and asked me to go out and pick them up for her. I asked why you couldn't do it, and she said it was because you were sleeping over at Jay's house. I said that was in no way possible since I had seen you at Bryan's house just last night, all tucked away in your little sleeping bag. Now she's pissed that you lied to her in the note you left."

"Why did you even tell her that? You're such a bitch!"

"Watch your mouth, Mac." Howard walks up behind us carrying two cups of hot chocolate. He hands one to Larissa. "That's my girlfriend you're talking to."

"Girlfriend?" Mac scoffs. "Dude, don't even start."

Howard steps close so that he is nose to nose with Mac, ready to fight. I look to Larissa and her devious smile. "Oh boys, calm yourselves down," she says. She grabs Howard's arm and pulls him toward her. "Anyways, Mac, you may as well go home and start your punishment early. Mom said you're grounded." With that, she and Howard walk away.

"I can't believe Howard right now," I say. "You better get going, though. I didn't mean to get you into so much trouble."

"You're worth it, man. You're my best friend." Mac looks back at the Valiselli siblings and their booth of oddities. "And whatever is up with them, we'll figure it out together."

We retrieve my bike and walk it out of the park. I

pop out the pegs on the back tires, and Mac climbs onto them and holds onto my shoulders as I ride toward his house. His dad is sitting in an Adirondack chair on the front porch, thumbing through the Sunday morning sports pages and sipping from a mug of coffee. He gives me a friendly nod, then meets Mac's eyes and shakes his head slowly.

"Better you than me in the doghouse," Mr. Alden calls out across the front yard to us. "Go get in there."

"See you at school tomorrow," I say. I watch Mac walk up to his house, knowing the difference in his family's version of punishment compared to mine when my dad was around. Mac will be just fine. Confined to his room with no TV for the afternoon at worst. Smirks from his dad and the inevitable "I'm not mad, I'm just hurt and disappointed in you" speech from his mom.

No bruises. No belts. No blood. Not like what happened at my house.

I wave to Mr. Alden, turn my bike around, and head back home.

Chapter Twelve
MAC

Math class and *first period* were four words that should not go together, but combined they described Mac's daily headache. He despised the subject, especially since his class was not allowed to use calculators this year. The school was experimenting with new curriculum, with half of the classes getting one textbook that encouraged the use of calculators, and the other half—including Mac's class—stuck with the archaic pencil-and-paper methods.

Mac had only two things to look forward to every morning on his way into first period. The first was his teacher, Ms. Linn. Despite the pure hatred he felt for the subject, he held no contempt for Ms. Linn. As far as teachers went, she was relatively young, in her late twenties and easy on the eyes. Mac had made a fool of himself three times already that year when she'd caught him staring at her. The other positive about the class was that Howard was in it.

At least, that was usually a positive. Mac was fully willing to forgive Howard for dating Larissa. He'd spent all Sunday afternoon and evening confined to his room, so he'd had a lot of time to cool off from his anger. Unfortunately, Howard was not ready to forgive Mac.

Howard walked into the classroom just after Mac sat down in his usual seat. Other than a few troublemakers that Ms. Linn forced to sit in the front row, the students didn't have assigned seats. Most kids gravitated toward the same seats every day regardless. Mac and Howard had staked a claim all year under the windows in the back corner of the room, which allowed them to trade notes or snacks throughout the period out of Ms. Linn's view. Today, however, tradition was broken. Howard kept his eyes averted from the back corner and instead made a beeline for a vacant seat in the second row, just between Daryl Collins in the third row and Jason Unger in the first.

Mac watched as Jason turned around and eyed Howard with confusion, followed by a glance back at Mac. Jason caught Mac staring back and flipped him the bird.

"Is there a problem, Mr. Unger?" Ms. Linn asked from right in front of him. She seemed to be the only teacher that wasn't afraid to challenge the oaf, and Jason took it from her because, like Mac, he found her stunning and only stuttered stupidly when he tried talking back to her.

"Uh, no, Ms. Linn," Jason muttered. "I thought Mackenzie threw something at me, that's all."

"Impressive aim from way in the back corner, Mr. Alden," Ms. Linn said to Mac as she shook her head and walked to the chalkboard to start her lesson. "Perhaps you should have tried out for the basketball team this year."

It was a throwaway interaction for her, Mac thought, but it would likely mean trouble for him if he crossed paths with Jason later in the day. He pushed the thought away, which wasn't difficult because Howard's avoidance consumed most of his mind. By the time the bell rang forty minutes later, he hadn't taken a single note in his binder about algebra.

There were two doors in the classroom, one near the front where Ms. Linn stood and one in the back of the room that was to always remain closed except in emergencies. Mac went for the latter door anyways.

"Mr. Alden, you know the rules about—" Ms. Linn's voice cut off as Mac sped through the doorway and slammed it shut.

It was too late.

Overgrown hands grabbed at his shirt collar. Jason's fingernails dug into the flesh of Mac's neck and shoulders as he launched Mac into a row of lockers. Lara Gionotti had her locker door ajar as she exchanged textbooks, and Mac's scalp sliced open on its edge. His body slammed into the remaining lockers with a *clunk* that echoed through the halls. He landed on his right side.

"That's for getting me in trouble in math class," Jason said. "And this one is payment for letting me borrow your bike and return it to the cage." His right foot slammed into Mac's crotch. For a moment, Mac thought the kick had just missed the goods by millimeters. Jason walked away and Mac pushed to his feet, and that's when he realized he'd been wrong. The blow had landed and the pain rushed in with delay. Mac keeled over and fell to the waxy linoleum in agony as kids shook their heads in pity and dispersed. Howard was among them, hesitating for just a moment before walking away with the rest.

"Good god, dude," Jay said as Mac writhed in pain on the floor.

"Let's get you up." Bryan was there. He grabbed Mac's left arm, forcing him to sit up, and Jay grasped the right side. They pulled him up to his feet and patted his back.

"What an asshole," Jay said.

Mac had trouble standing straight. He hunched over with his hands on his knees. "It's nothing new," he said with a strained voice. "Jason's never going to change."

"Jason? I was talking about Howard. Did you see how he just watched and walked away? Cold, man. Cold."

"I wanted to forgive him today. I mean, I still will. If he likes my sister, what's the big deal?" Mac pushed through the pain and stood up as straight as he could. The warning bell rang out. "We better get to class."

They walked toward history class, the one period all four friends shared. "Maybe if he dropped to his knees and begged. I'd probably tell him to kiss my Jordans. Better those than your sister," Jay said.

"Get over it, man," Bryan said. "You had no chance with Larissa anyways."

"Maybe Violeta, then," Jay said with renewed hope.

"She's too into Mac. Sorry to shoot down your dreams again."

Mac pretended not to hear Bryan. He was fifteen years old and still terrified of girls. Of the group, Bryan had started young with his first relationship—if you could even call it that—in the sixth grade with Marissa Ellis. He'd had a few other girlfriends in seventh grade, though the girls had become as weird around him as anyone else since his father's prison sentence. Jay and Mac had no experience whatsoever with the ladies, nor had Howard until whenever the fling with Larissa had started.

The boys just made it to the doorway of their history class as the bell rang. Mac looked around the room and it was just what he'd expected. Howard had already settled near the front of the room, all the desks around him occupied. Sandy Wilson had been displaced from her usual desk by Howard's breaking of the unofficial seating protocols, throwing the entire room out of balance. She took the seat normally occupied by Mark Hansen, so he was at Mac's usual desk. Mark's best friend Aaron Giles had followed him, so he took Bryan's regular position in the corner. And so on... Madness.

By the time Mac, Jay, and Bryan had settled into open desks, they were dispersed all around the room. All three shot glares at the back of Howard's head, but the would-be anarchist never once turned around to witness the chaos he had created.

Mr. Sutter lectured on the spread of the plague in Europe, which Mac would normally have found fascinating, but all he could think about was the pain in his groin and how much Howard seemed to bask in everything falling apart.

By the time the clock marked 11:50 AM and the bell rang to start lunch, Mac was able to stand mostly straight without shooting pains from his midsection. If that was getting better, he hoped, then perhaps things with Howard would cool off as well. They didn't share any classes in third or fourth period, so maybe that time away from each other would work miracles.

Mac retrieved his brown bag from his locker and peeked in at the contents on his way to the lunch patio behind the school. An apple, a ham and American cheese sandwich on a chewy French roll, one of those granola bar packets with two bars as hard as rocks that crumble into a thousand pieces when you take the first bite, a can of root beer, and one of the packs of Shark Bites that Larissa and Violeta had purchased from the grocery store on Saturday. It was pretty much the same lunch he ate every day, but he wouldn't have had it any other way. He pushed through the back doors and looked around as he descended the four steps onto the back patio. Howard was usually first out, as the band room was accessed from the back of the school and he was able to stow away his viola in the instrument cabinet and rush out to grab their usual table as soon as the bell rang. This time, however, the table was empty.

Mac scanned the nearby picnic tables and benches, but Howard was nowhere to be seen.

"Over there," a voice said. Mac turned to face Jay at the top of the steps. He was pointing toward the opposite side of the patio. Mac followed the direction of Jay's finger to where the juniors and seniors congregated during lunch. "Abandoning us yet again, the traitor."

Over at one of the tables, Howard sat with his arm around Larissa, surrounded by Larissa's friends and their boyfriends. Mac realized then that Howard appeared to fit in with that crowd. They had accepted him seemingly without question, a sophomore among juniors. He laughed at their jokes, added to their conversations, got them to chuckle at his own sarcastic banter.

"Sick, isn't it?" Violeta had come down the steps at

some point as Mac stared in bewilderment at his lost pal. He turned to her in confusion.

"Larissa's your best friend," Mac said. "Why would you say that?"

"She gets a certain way when she has a boyfriend. Ignores me. Pushes me away. She gets all sarcastic and makes all kinds of little quips about me to make herself look better."

"Come sit with us, then!" Jay offered. Mac thought the desperation in his voice was a little pathetic. "We have plenty of room over at our..."

He trailed off and Mac saw why. Over at their normal spot, Jason Unger and a couple of his goons sat on the splintered wood tabletop, their filthy sneakers muddying up the benches.

"Looks like you boys have enough change to deal with. I'll just go subject myself to Her Majesty over there." Violeta gave a playful slap on Mac's shoulder. "Don't worry. I'll make sure she doesn't chew him up and spit him out." With that, she walked through the crowd toward Larissa and Howard.

"Where's Bryan?" Mac asked Jay. They both looked around the yard but couldn't pick him out among the crowds of students. Mac decided Bryan wasn't out there and climbed the steps. He gestured for Jay to follow him back inside the school.

"Maybe we should check the bathrooms. Could be a bad case of diarrhea," Jay offered. "You know how that boy eats. One too many fried foods and your insides turn to mush. This one time, I had bad sausage on a slice of pizza from Dominick's downtown. We should have stuck to the Hut, but my dad really wanted to try something new, and Mr. Dominick is a patient of his. All I could think of while I was stuck on the porcelain throne was that my dad must have given him some bad medical treatment at some point and this was his revenge."

Jay reached into his own brown bag and retrieved a slice of leftover pizza. He took a bite and chewed loudly as they walked down the hall in search of their friend. Mac couldn't help but laugh. Jay had a way of brightening up the mood even when he hadn't intended on being funny.

They didn't need to go far. The first boys' room door they pushed open revealed exactly who they were looking for. Bryan jumped as Jay kicked the door open. "Never touch a bathroom door if you can avoid it," Jay said through a mouthful of cheese and pepperoni, "unless you want to kick off a new plague like the one Mr. Sutter talked about—hey there's Bryan!"

Mac followed him into the bathroom. "Everything okay, Bry?" His question was answered for him without any further words uttered.

"What the hell?" Jay asked at the sight of the sink Bryan hunched over. The bottom half of Jay's pizza slice slipped from the aluminum foil and splattered face-down on the soiled linoleum at his feet. "Damn it!"

Mac rushed forward and peered into the sink. The

grimy porcelain was covered in clumps of hair, stuck in coagulated loogies and other filth that normally basted the edges of the sinks in any of the boys' bathrooms around the school. Without asking for permission, Mac reached up and rubbed at the side of Bryan's head. "Dude, what is happening right now? I thought it was just a little bit of hair yesterday." The right side of Bryan's head was patchy, clumps of remaining hair spotted with misshapen circles of flesh. Mac stepped behind Bryan and noted the same on the back of his head and an identical looking left side.

"I have a hat in my locker," Jay offered. He chucked the remains of his brown bag into the trash can, making a soft *thud* among the soggy paper towels, and ran out of the bathroom.

"What am I going to do, Mac? I'll be bald by the weekend if this keeps up."

"Maybe we really should get you to Jay's dad like I said yesterday. He can run some kind of tests, figure out what's wrong."

"No. It's being caused by *them*. Doctor Patel's tests won't show anything wrong. He'll probably send me to yet another shrink who will say I'm pulling out my hair as a reaction to the stress of my dad or some bullshit like that. I need to figure out something else."

Mac stood speechless. It broke his heart to see his friend descend further into delusions about bright lights from spaceships, alien night visitors, hillbillies in pickup trucks driving him around under a tarp and returning him home early in the morning. None of it made sense except that maybe the psychologists were right. Trauma wormed its way deep within Mac's best friend and poisoned his heart and soul.

"I'd do anything to take all this away for you," Mac said. A part of him hoped nobody was hiding out in one of the stalls to hear his words. The last thing he needed was for someone to spread rumors around school that he was professing his love to Bryan in the bathroom. The other part of him didn't care. His best friend needed his support now. Reputation be damned. "I'd trade places in a heartbeat if it meant these things would stop coming for you, or if it meant your dad could never hurt you again. You don't deserve any of it."

"Got it!" Jay called out as he busted through the door. He thrusted the hat at Bryan.

"Chicago Bulls?" Mac asked. "You know Bryan doesn't give a crap about basketball."

"It'll cover the weirdness on his head, birdbrain," Jay shot back.

"It's great. I appreciate it," Bryan said. He slipped the hat over his head. "A bit tight, but I'll make it work." Once he got it in place, it covered most of the bald patches, but some around his ears were still visible. On the back of his head, the gap at the adjustable snap band acted like a window into one of the bigger rear patches. Mac locked eyes with Jay, indicating both boys saw it, but neither had the heart to tell Bryan.

"It was a good idea," Mac admitted to Jay. "Nobody will know what's happening, Bry."

Bryan washed the hair down the drain and the boys exited the bathroom.

"And you're right, Bryan," Mac said. "It's time we do something to put an end to whatever is happening to you. Nobody messes with one of us."

Chapter Thirteen
MAC

Mac darted to the bike cage as soon as the final bell of the day rang out. He scanned the collection, but his wasn't there despite what Jason had said just before the kick in the nuts.

"Need a ride?" Violeta asked as she walked among the mob of juniors and seniors toward the student parking lot. "I've got enough room in the car. I'm sure your sister and her new boy-toy will take the back seat.

"No thanks," Mac said, unable to tell if the heat in his cheeks was from blushing at Violeta's offer or anger over the thought of Howard and Larissa locking lips in the back seat.

"Better find a ladder, then," she said. Seeing his confusion, she pointed up before walking away. Mac tilted his head to find the state flag had been replaced. Dangling twenty-five feet in the air, Mac's bike hung limply as a corpse in the gallows of a western film.

"Son of a bitch," he whispered. He walked over to the pole and analyzed the rope. It had been tied sloppily around the two protruding pegs. Instead of a clean white, something brown was caked all over the knots of the nylon rope. One sniff told him it was dog shit. "Son of a bitch," he repeated.

"Let me help," Bryan said on his approach. He walked over to a nearby trash can, pulled out a couple discarded brown paper lunch bags, and used them as gloves. He winced as the dog crap squished through the thin paper covering his hands. "Grab a little higher on the rope. It'll move fast under the weight of your bike."

Mac nodded and reached just above the smeared poop. He gripped tightly as Bryan undid the knots. They worked the rope hand-over-hand to lower the bike the first few feet before they were interrupted.

"Oh Leslie and Mackenzie!" a singsong voice called out. "Catch this!"

Both boys turned toward the sound of Jason Unger's voice only to see him lob two flaming paper bags at them. They didn't need to ask what was in them. Wherever Jason had procured the dog turds he'd smeared on the ropes, he'd clearly found even more of the stuff and filled the sacks. Bryan and Mac released their grips on the rope simultaneously to swat away the incoming incendiary poo-bombs, and Mac's bike came crashing down with a heartbreaking *thud* on the pavement. Jason laughed as he walked away, but all Mac could do was stare in shock at the remains of his bicycle. The front tire had popped off. The frame bent about thirty degrees, now only fit to ride in an awkward circle at best. The chain snapped into several pieces. The bike was no more than fodder for a trash heap.

Jay arrived just as a crowd of onlookers dispersed. "What does that boy have against bicycles?" he asked. "Such a brute."

Bryan and Jay unchained their own bikes and wheeled them out of the cage. Mac left his wreckage sprawled on the concrete under the flagpole for the janitors to clean up and ambled over to a bench. His friends followed and sat on their bikes, facing him.

"So, what do we do now?" Bryan asked.

"Get our driver's licenses for starters," Jay said.

"I wish I could run that asshole down in a car," Mac said. He lifted his head and faced his remaining friends, ignoring the tears in his eyes. "That's still over a year away, though, and we have a more immediate problem right now. We have to stop whatever is happening to Bryan. That's our number one priority."

A devious look formed on Jay's face. "I say we blow them up!"

Bryan rolled his eyes. "Yeah, and who is going to get us the explosives?"

"It's not like we need professional bombs," Jay replied. "How about Molotov cocktails? They do it in the movies all the time."

"Burn those suckers to a crisp," Mac said. "Honestly

not a bad idea. Even just distracting them could work, and then we rush them."

"Pew pew!" Jay made the high pitch noises along with his finger guns aimed at Mac. "They'll fry us with laser pistols before we can even touch them, I bet."

Both boys turned to Bryan, who shrugged. "Never seen evidence of weapons, but if they're advanced enough to fly around in spaceships, I wouldn't put it past them. Anyways, I don't think it's going to work. When they come, it's like everything around me freezes. I can't even move. The lights they use are more than just visual. More like a sticky mass that tranquilizes whatever is in its path."

"We just need to strike fast," Jay suggested. "Hide in another room until the lights come, then kick the door in and strike."

"What about fireworks to distract them. Maybe those will even throw off their ship's sensors, send them crashing down." Mac felt foolish even suggesting such a thing, but they had nothing to lose. If aliens were indeed coming for his best friend in the night, reality had already fallen to the wayside.

"That's not a bad idea, Mac. But where do we get fireworks in October?"

Bryan chimed in. "Maybe Howard?"

"The turncoat?" Jay replied. "Fat chance. The man hates us."

"What, you guys think just because I'm Chinese

American, I'll have an endless supply of illegal fireworks in my garage just waiting to be used?"

The guys turned around to face their recently estranged friend. When nobody replied to his question, Howard's offended look morphed into a smile. "I'm just playing with you. You know my parents always stash away a few cases for Lunar New Year. What do we need them for?"

Mac filled him in while Jay glowered at him with crossed arms. When they finished, Howard locked eyes with Jay.

"You aren't going to forgive me? Listen, I know you've always had the hots for Larissa, but she doesn't feel the same way. There'll be someone out there for you who does. You're the funniest and most loyal guy I know." Howard turned his eyes to Mac. "And dude, I'm sorry I didn't make sure you were cool with me dating your sister. She makes me really happy, but not as much our friendship does. I'd end it with her if it meant staying friends with you guys."

"It's okay, Howard. I'm over it. I know my sister, though. She'll tear out your heart sooner or later just to see it splattered on the sidewalk, but I'll still be here for you."

"Me too," Jay added, "unless she needs a shoulder to cry on when it's done. Then I'll be there for her instead."

Howard turned to Bryan. "I'm sorry I wasn't there

for you with whatever happened the night of our sleepover. You don't deserve what's happening to you. I'm here for you now, I promise. Give me some skin and call it even?"

He held out his hand, palm up. Bryan reached out and rubbed his hand along Howard's. "Water under the bridge, brother." Bryan eyed all his friends, then did a double take at the arrival of the principal, Mr. Edwards. "Let's get out of here. We can go back to my house. Mom will be at work again, so we can finish planning there."

Mac once again rode the pegs of Bryan's bike as the crew passed through town. The sky was clear, and Mac soaked in the late afternoon sun as his hair blew with the breeze. Despite the tension between the friends over the last few days, and despite the barrage of assaults from Jason Unger, everything felt right. The gang was back together. They had the beginnings of a plan to help Bryan's problem. Nothing else could possibly go wrong for them.

And then Bryan's house came into view.

At the sight of a police cruiser parked behind Mrs. Adams's car, Bryan skidded to a halt in the middle of the road. Jay and Howard swerved off to either side and applied their own brakes to stop alongside him. Mac hopped off the pegs and stood to Bryan's right.

"Drug bust, I bet," Jay said. The other three boys turned to him and stared in bewilderment. He shrugged his shoulders. "What? Maybe Mrs. A has an illicit job on the side we don't know about. She could be running drugs at night when she says she's working graveyard at the diner. How cool would that be?"

"Jay, please listen to me as I say this with the utmost respect and humility: you are a complete and utter moron. Shut the hell up," Howard said, then nodded to Bryan as if giving him permission to take whatever action he felt necessary.

Without speaking or waiting for Mac to get back onto the pegs, Bryan took off and pedaled toward his house.

"Alright then, we ride straight into the hands of the law," Jay said. He brought one foot onto his pedal, just about to follow Bryan's path when Mac stretched an arm out and grabbed Jay's shoulder.

"Just give him a minute." They watched as Bryan sped home.

"Mom?" Bryan's voice reached them even over the distance as he approached the porch and dropped his bike next to the police car. "Mom, what's happening?"

"Mac, we have to be with him," Howard said. Mac nodded, and the three of them rushed toward the house, with Mac sprinting on foot just behind the other two and their bikes. As they looked ahead at their friend, they saw the front door open. Mac recognized Officer Malone, one of the few cops on the small local police force and the officer that often assisted at events at their school. Even from a distance, Mac made out the look of pity Malone gave at the sight of Bryan's arrival.

"What's going on?" Bryan yelled at the officer. "Did something happen to my mom?"

Jay, Howard, and Mac arrived just behind Bryan, who didn't turn around to acknowledge them. The cop looked over the boys.

"Mr. Adams," Officer Malone said. "Bryan, I mean. I'm sorry if this comes as a surprise, but there was a court date today and it was decided by the judge that Karl Adams—I mean, your father—would be released on parole."

"What the hell are you talking about?" Bryan asked. "My mom would have told me about the parole hearing. She didn't say anything!" He jumped toward the porch, but Officer Malone stepped to the side to block him. "What are you doing?"

"Bryan, please listen to me," Malone said in a soft voice. "Your mom didn't think there was a chance he'd be let out, so she did not want to burden you with any worries."

"Then why is he here?"

"The judge heard him out, spoke to the warden and head guards and even your mom. Everyone raved about how he's been a model prisoner with a perfect behavioral record. He met all the criteria to be let out early."

"The man is a monster," Mac chimed in.

Jay added, "Yeah, he's a real asshole."

"He's just going to hurt us again," Bryan said.

A look of guilt flashed over Officer Malone's face. "If he as much as lays a finger on you or your mom, you come tell me and I'll make sure he is back in prison for violating the terms of his parole."

"But why did he come back? Mom and I testified against him and got him locked up in the first place. He's going to kill us."

"He's not going to hurt you. I can guarantee it. Besides, your mom never sought out a restraining order against him. This house and the land are in his name. If anything, it's your mom that he can ask to leave if he wants, but I don't think it will come to that. There's no choice, Bryan, unless he violates his terms."

"So they just wait for him to hurt them?" Howard asked. He spit just in front of Malone's boots. "Do you all get paid on commission for house calls or something? Just waiting for something bad to happen before you come out and take him back to jail?"

Malone looked hurt. "Listen, son, it's not like that at all. We're bound by the rules as much as anyone. All you can be right now is supportive of your buddy. I'm sorry I can't do more."

With that, Officer Malone squeezed past the boys to his cruiser. He started the engine and gave one last look of regret before driving away. The front door opened. Karl Adams stepped out onto the porch. Mac had grown up seeing the man, always afraid of the evil so apparent behind his stare. Something about him always reminded Mac of the Big Bad Wolf in the old Disney

Three Little Pigs cartoon. Mac had several nightmares as a younger child about the man, one minute his best friend's dad, the next a wolf trying to bite their heads clean off with needle sharp teeth.

"Come on up here, you little shit," Karl said to his son with a redneck's sense of humor. "Give your old man a hug."

Mac didn't know why he did it, but he reached over to Bryan as if he could stop the proceedings, turn Bryan around, and ride out of here to safety. Bryan brushed him off, took a deep breath, and stepped up onto the porch. He stopped in front of his father, arms down at his side. Mr. Adams grunted out a laugh, grasped Bryan's shoulders in his tattooed fingers, and pulled the boy in for a hug. Bryan's arms remained down, and Mac didn't think it was lost on the man. Karl stood there with his arms around his son regardless, his eyes closed.

Then his eyes opened and met Mac's. He winked at the boy, but it wasn't playful in any way. The maliciousness shot out at Mac like a spark of electricity. Mac stumbled back a step and twisted his foot on a loose piece of gravel, causing his attention to shift away from Bryan and his dad. When he looked back up, Mr. Adams had turned toward the door, pushed it opened, and guided Bryan through. In the dim interior, Mac could just make out Mrs. Adams. Her face was flush with tears and fear.

Bryan didn't turn around to say goodbye to his friends. His posture oozed pure terror.

"So long, boys," Karl called out to the kids before closing the front door on them.

The boys stood there in shock for what felt like minutes. They turned and looked at each other, then hurried away from Bryan's house helpless and dejected.

Chapter Fourteen
BRYAN

I meet mom's eyes as I step into the house and my heart is broken. We just stare at each other. I know it's only a couple seconds at most, but it feels like hours. The shadows close in as Dad pushes the door closed behind me, shutting me off from not just the sun but the entire world outside of these walls. Away from safety. Away from my friends.

"So here we are," Dad says. Mom's eyes widen as the panic takes hold of her. "One big happy family, reunited." I don't turn to face him, even though my fear gives him more power over me. "My own flesh and blood, and my old ball-and-chain. Ha. That last one takes on a new meaning after where I've been these last three years. After where you two sent me."

"Can... Can I get you a beer?" Mom asks. She sounds tiny in a way I haven't heard in over three years.

Dad pushes past me, bumping his shoulder against

mine. I don't know if it is intentional, but I assume so. The first warning to me of what is to come. "You know, a beer does sound nice. Don't tell me you've been keeping them cold for me all this time, though. You didn't think I was coming home so soon."

"I think there is still a case in the rear of the pantry from back before..." Mom trails off and scurries away like a mouse toward the kitchen.

"Back before our little Judas here testified against me in court," Dad finishes for her. I finally manage to break my stillness and move my head. My eyes meet Dad's hateful stare. "But that's all water under the bridge now, ain't it, you little shit?" His glare burns into me like a laser, and then his face contorts as a smile breaks out. "Come on now, where's your sense of humor, squirt?"

Dad walks into the living room and plops down into the recliner that he's always favored. It was once a light tan color, browned over years of his after-work sweat soaking into it, and then from the dust that fell there since his arrest. Mom and I never once sat in it during his three years away. It smells too much like him. Sickening. Rotten. A cloud of dust poofs into the air as he plops down. Dad coughs.

"Well shit, do you and your mom not clean anything around here?" he asks while waving away the airborne dust around his face. "You sure didn't keep up the grounds out there. Going to break our backs just bringing those fields back to life."

I stand in the hallway just watching him in silence. Mom brushes past me and sets a glass of ice on the coffee table. She cracks open a can of light beer and pours it over the ice. The head of foam grows exponentially as the beer meets the cubes and overflows the rim before Mom realizes and cuts off the pour.

"Spill it all over the table, why don't you?" Dad reaches out and gives Mom what would be a playful tap on the rear from any loving couple. With him, though, it's more of a threat.

"Don't touch her."

I don't say it loud, but it reaches Dad's ears anyway as he bends forward to grab the glass off the table. He pauses for a moment, then resumes his action and lifts the glass to his lips. He sips the foam loudly, something he would have slapped me across the face for doing when I was younger. He lets out a loud *aahhh* to demonstrate how refreshing the beer is.

Mom is above him, watching as he takes a couple more sips. "I'm glad I saved those for you," she says. "Still good after all this time."

He looks at her, then holds the beer up to the light and observes it like a jeweler inspecting a diamond. "Still good?" Now that he's cleared the head of foam, he takes a big gulp of the lager. He coughs. "That's going a little overboard. It's like drinking piss that's been soaking up the heat in a jar on the dashboard of a car in August in the middle of Death Valley." He looks around at Mom's face and then mine. We show no emotion.

"What, did someone die? I'm just making jokes here. Lighten the hell up."

I watch him for another few seconds and then turn toward the stairs and take another step.

"Leslie, where are you going?" Mom calls after me. The desperation in her voice breaks my heart, but I suppress my feelings.

"Homework," I yell as I stomp up the stairs. I hate myself more with each step I take because I know Mom is terrified and wants me there to protect her. I'm a coward and I leave her with that monster instead.

I WAKE UP FULLY CLOTHED, SPRAWLED OUT ON TOP OF my lumpy blankets and a half-written essay. The fact that I can move on my own tells me it wasn't the unwelcome night visitors that woke me up, but a light shines through my window regardless. I glance at my digital alarm clock, the red numbers displaying 10:26 PM. I peek out the window to see Mom's car idling for a couple seconds before pulling away from the house and down the driveway.

She's going to work late? I wonder. *Or maybe driving herself to the hospital after Dad had his way with her, taking revenge on her for sending him to prison. That would mean I'm next.*

Instead of sitting and waiting for the attack, I decide to face him head on. I straighten my rumpled clothing and head out of my room. I stop halfway down the stairs as I hear sniffling.

"Mom?"

"Hi, honey," she calls back in a feigned cheery tone. "You missed dinner. Can I fix you something?"

I resume my descent and look around when I arrive at the first-floor landing. Mom sits on the loveseat, a pile of tissues on the cushion next to her. She follows my gaze and brushes the blood-soaked items against her thigh.

"Nosebleeds," she says. "Used to get them all the time. It's been a while."

"He hit you already?" I step into the living room for a better look at her, wondering if her face will be bruised, her nose newly crooked. Mom puts on a fake smile like a preschool teacher trying to explain something to a three-year-old.

"Oh no, my love. Your father is so happy to be home. He's not going to mess that up now that he has his freedom back."

"Right." I turn my back on her and walk to the kitchen. The remnants of the six pack are strewn on the table around takeout containers from the diner. There are more containers than usual, and they hadn't been in the fridge this morning. Mom must have brought these home from the diner while I was at school. As if she were expecting company. I call back toward the living room. "Did you know he was coming? Did you know Dad was getting out?"

Silence lingers for a few moments. Another sniffle breaks it, then the blowing of bloody snot into another tissue. I walk back into the living room to face her.

"Why didn't you warn me?" I ask. "Why didn't you prepare me?"

"I'm sorry, Leslie. When I went to his parole hearing last week, he—"

"You went to his hearing? You've known since last week and didn't say a word?"

Mom goes on, trying her best to placate me. "—he expressed his remorse to the judge. He promised everyone in the court, and me, that his dark days were behind him. He guaranteed that he wouldn't hurt us ever again."

"How could you buy that?" I drop down onto the couch across from her and put one shoe up on the coffee table. I pull it away quickly, knowing Dad would deck me for that if he walked back through the front door. "After everything we've been through..."

"If you had seen him there, you'd understand. How frail he's gotten while he's been locked away. His eyes were sad, but hopeful. There was nothing in him that looked threatening."

I know she's lying. I saw the fear in her when I came home from school. It broke my heart then, and it breaks my heart now to see how hard she tries to justify everything. She always made excuses for him, and she's already doing it again.

"Just give him another chance," she pleads. "If he

hurts you again, we'll tell his parole officer. He'll be right back in that cell, and he knows it."

I stare at her for a minute, a confusing blend of rage and pity and sadness and terror running through me.

"Is he out drinking?" I ask.

"He wanted to see his old friends and celebrate his release," she says. That's all I need to hear to know he'll come home completely wasted, and then it's a fifty-fifty chance he'll either be violent against one of us or black out on the couch until halfway through tomorrow.

I pray for the latter.

Mom gets up from her tissue-covered loveseat, gathers her trash into a bundle, and motions for me to follow her into the kitchen. She tosses the crimson tissues, washes her hands, and makes me a plate of chicken tenders and steak fries. I don't bother with the bottle of ketchup she sets on my placemat. It looks too much like what was coming from her nose in the other room just a few minutes ago.

After I eat, I kiss Mom on the cheek, say goodnight, and go back to my room. I promise myself I'll brush my teeth in the morning. I just want this day to end.

I toss and turn for an hour, unable to slow my heart rate and relax enough to escape into slumber. The last time I recall glancing at my clock is 1:30 AM. Just as I am finally about to drift off to sleep, the lights come. They're accompanied by the crunching of gravel under the tires of a car. It's Dad, not the others. In the dead of night, the sound of his boots staggering up the walkway carries up to my room. He throws the door open too hard and it bashes against the wall, then he slams it closed without regard for his sleeping family. The bastard stomps through the kitchen, rustles through the refrigerator, then gives up with a loud curse when he apparently can't find anything worth eating. He walks around downstairs some more. I wait for his footsteps up the stairs, but they never come. I realize he passed out on the couch after all.

Safety ensured for the night, I allow myself to relax and fall back to sleep.

Until the lights come again. This time, they're not car headlights at all. For once, I don't know which is worse.

Chapter Fifteen
BRYAN

I awake the next morning in my bed to the sounds of shock-jock deejays performing prank calls. I kick my way out of the warmth of my comforter and reach over to turn off the radio alarm on my clock. I look around before realization dawns on me.

I'm in my room.

I know I saw the lights in the middle of the night, but as hard as I try, I can't pull up any memories beyond that. It's not so unusual that I can't recall what happened during those night visits, but usually I can at least grasp a remnant for a few seconds before it disappears like water down the drain. Today, though, there is nothing at all.

I pull on fresh underwear and socks as well as the pair of jeans I wore yesterday, which still has another three or four days before I need to find other pants to wear, barring any stains. My dresser drawers are nearly empty, so I reach into the mound of clothes on my floor and pull out the first three t-shirts I can find. I give them all the sniff test and toss the two most unbearable shirts back on the pile.

Down the hall, Mom's bedroom door is open and the bed is vacant and neatly made. I tiptoe down the stairs, knowing better than to wake Dad when he's in his usual hangover state. I've had years of training on that, and even his three-year absence hasn't erased it from my memory. I peek into the living room.

"What?" I whisper.

"Did you say something?" Mom calls from the kitchen. I take a second glance around the room to make sure he's not there, perhaps passed out on the floor, but the room is indeed empty. I turn and trek to the kitchen.

Mom is at the stove, one hand on the handle of a pot, the other waving a wooden spoon in my direction. "Sit down," she says, motioning the spoon toward the table. I follow the direction and see a glass of orange juice waiting for me at my usual seat. "Oatmeal is almost finished, and then you better head out the door before you're late for school."

"But where's Dad?" I can't help but ask. A look flashes over Mom's face, somewhere between fear and shame.

"I told you last night, he went out with his friends.

You remember how that can go. Sometimes gone for two or three days. It's just who he is, Leslie."

"But he came back last night. I heard him at 1:30. The car is out front." A maroon glare from the car parked right outside of the window shines in with the morning sun.

Mom peers through the steam emanating from the pot of oatmeal as she walks toward the table with it. "He must have gotten a ride to the bar last night," she says. A clear tinge of annoyance rings out in her voice and spills over onto her facial expression. She plops two heaping spoons full of the mush into my bowl. It's already been mixed with the brown sugar, cinnamon, and dried cranberries. She serves herself some of the oats and leaves the rest for Dad, then returns the pot to the stovetop. She comes back to the table and we eat in silence.

I shovel the last spoonful into my mouth when I hear Dad's footsteps coming up the gravel driveway and onto the porch. The door creaks open, much slower than when he'd come home last night, and closes just as gently. Mom puts on a smile as Dad steps into the kitchen. I take a deep breath, then turn to face him, determined to start the day on his good side.

"Good morn—"

I stop, the look on his face telling me I should quit while I'm ahead. He looks like he's just seen a gruesome murder in front of his eyes. He glances at our bowls, then at the stove. Without a word, he walks over and grabs the pot. He stands over the range and uses the wooden spoon to consume the congealing oatmeal. Stray oats run down his chin, the liquified brown sugar leaving a disgusting trail.

"Honey, did you have a good time?" Mom asks him in her sweetest voice. His eyes stare off into the wall, his daze not broken by mom's question. He just remains there, chewing and swallowing and shoveling more into his mouth.

After a few awkward minutes, I risk breaking the calm. I down the rest of the orange juice—wincing at the taste of freezer burn from the canned frozen concentrate Mom used to make it—and rise to my feet. Three steps toward the doorway, Dad's stupor breaks behind me and I stop in my tracks.

"Where do you think you're going?" His voice is level, but I've known him long enough to know the cadence of his speech hides fire. He's ready to spit it at me like a dragon.

"Honey, he has school," Mom starts, but Dad slams the wooden spoon down against the rim of the pot.

"I'm asking him," he says to her, then turns his eyes on me. "Where the fuck are you going?"

"It's only Tuesday," I say. "Still have four days of school left for the week."

Dad picks up the pot and hurls it across the kitchen. It slams into the refrigerator, the remaining contents sticking to the white metal doors like boogers. "You're my kid. You have as many days left as I say you do. I don't care if it's Tuesday or Saturday, you aren't going anywhere until we get the land back in working order. It's what you lazy pieces of shit should have been doing for the past thirty-six months. You're dumb as a rock, boy. I don't even know why you bother with school. Your place is here, and even after I die, you'll be tethered to this farm, so you had better get a head start and make it produce for us now!"

"Oh, Karl," Mom says. She jumps out of her chair and hurries over to Dad. "I don't work until this afternoon. I have plenty of time to help while Leslie goes to school."

I know something is coming and I want to run forward and pull Mom back, but I'm a coward. I'm under his spell. My feet are glued to the stained kitchen linoleum. Dad's arms don't lift, though. Instead, he sucks in his phlegm, then spits out a chunky wad right in Mom's face. Saliva and snot and chewed oatmeal splatter on her forehead and she stops in her tracks.

"Things are going to change around here," he growls. "It's bad enough I have to live here with you two Judases. Now I have to revive this fucking farm with your worthless help. This is all your own doing!" He pushes past Mom, not striking her with fists or the back of his hand, but shoving her aside with his shoulder. I step back as he storms past me. He climbs the stairs toward their room and yells back down. "Meet me in the barn in five minutes, boy. I'm putting your worthless ass to work!"

I turn away from Mom, not able to face her shame, and walk out the front door toward the barn.

There will be no more school for me today. Maybe not this whole week.

There will be no escape.

Chapter Sixteen

MAC

C amellia Flats didn't have a first-run movie theater. No fancy restaurants and very few fast-food chains. Certainly no malls or even name brand outlets. Residents had to drive half an hour away to Raventree Hollow for those things, or even farther to the big city. One thing Camellia Flats *did* have that Raventree Hollow didn't was Galactic Dragon Fun Center. In a town so lacking in entertainment options, Galactic Dragon stood out, an ensemble of neon laser lights shooting out into the otherwise bland town's night sky.

The outdoors portion included three miniature golf courses to choose from, utilizing an epic fantasy theme with dragons and knights and castles. Indoors, an arcade with colorful screens and all the audible *bleeps* and *bloops* of the most recent video games brought the town into the present or even the future with its outer-space science fiction themes and flashing lights. The most recent addition was a laser tag arena filled with blacklight projections, pounding electronica music, and more excitement than the rest of the town combined could provide.

For the teens of Camellia Flats, Galactic Dragon was a caffeine-filled heaven, a sugar-high paradise. That is, when the kids had enough allowance saved up to spend at the place, which wasn't the cheapest form of entertainment for all its attractions and snack bar goodies.

Fortunately, Jay, Howard, Bryan, and Mac had saved up for this night for quite some time. Jay's birthday had come and gone in the middle of the school week, so his father had loaded him up with a hundred dollars to spend in lieu of a birthday party. Jay had planned to buy rounds of golf and laser tag and even a couple pizzas to share with his best friends, but his friends were on the hook for any extra rounds or arcade games they wanted to play. The only problem, however, was that one from their quartet had been missing in action all week.

"I can't believe Bryan didn't show," Jay said through bites of cheesy breadsticks. "I only turn fifteen once."

The party hadn't gone all downhill, however. When it was clear that Howard was going to be mopey without his girlfriend, along with the empty seat normally reserved for Bryan, Jay caved in and gave Howard permission to invite Larissa along. Mac's first instinct was to protest, but he bit his tongue to preserve their friendship. Besides, Larissa had been uncharacteristically cheerful all week, even amenable toward Mac. Howard clearly made her a happier person.

"Where are the ladies, anyway?" Jay asked, dropping a greasy ball of napkins onto his plate. "The cheese has coagulated, the breadstick oils have dried up, and this pitcher of cola is mostly melted ice."

"That's my sister, late as always," Mac said, then shot a glance at Howard to make sure he wasn't upset at the comment. "I mean, she's probably dolling herself up for Howard."

"Women," Jay said. Howard reached under the table and fumbled with something. Mac and Jay met eyes with a confused look and turned to Howard. "Shake it once, it's okay. Shake it twice, you're playing with yourself."

"Seriously, what are you doing under there?" Mac asked.

Howard pulled his hand up above the table and showed the other guys what he held. "Just checking if she tried to get ahold of me."

"You have a beeper?" Jay asked.

"When did you get a pager?" Mac asked. "And why?"

"It's my dad's, but he never uses it. Just sits in his roll-top desk under all the bills and junk mail. You know how he loves his technology, at least for the first few days of owning it." Howard shrugged his shoulders. "Besides, Larissa was on me about never being near a phone when she wants to talk since I'm always out riding around with you guys."

After Monday's disaster with Mac's bike, he'd gone home and cleaned up Larissa's old six-speed that had been collecting dust and mouse piss in the garage. It had glittery purple and gold designs on the frame, but otherwise had been practically unused since their dad had gifted it to Larissa for her thirteenth birthday party. She hadn't wanted it and had barely touched it aside from a couple rides around the neighborhood to placate their dad. Mac ignored the taunts from the guys about the color scheme, hiked the seat up as high as it would go, cut off the tassels, and made it his own.

"So did she page you?" Mac asked.

"Nah—oh, there she is!" Howard jumped out of the corner booth and jogged through the crowd to the doors, where Larissa and Violeta had entered and froze, letting their eyes adjust to the bright flashing lights of the place.

"Perhaps this is my chance to make a move on Violeta," Jay said with a confidence that Mac could not figure out the origin of. He turned to Mac and spread his lips wide, teeth together. "Quick, do I have any pizza in my teeth?"

"Nah, you're good," Mac replied, ignoring the little green fleck of parsley or basil protruding front and center. "Good luck, man."

Jay slid out of the booth and Mac watched as Violeta gave him a friendly hug. "There's the big birthday boy," she said in a playful manner. Jay and Howard directed the girls over to the booth.

"Ladies first," Jay said. Mac found himself scooting all the way back, enclosed on one side by Larissa and Howard and the other side by Violeta and Jay.

"It's Friday night, Mac," Violeta said, punching his shoulder playfully. "And we're in the happiest place on earth—or at least in this dump of a town. Why do you look so dour?"

"He misses his Bry-Bry-Baby," Larissa said in a sad baby voice to mock him, her lower lip held out in a pout. She rolled her eyes and continued in her normal voice. "Seriously, where is that boy? At home crying to sad songs or something?"

"Shove off," Mac replied. "We're here for Jay's birthday. Don't be such a—"

"Who wants to golf?" Howard cut in. "Jay is paying!"

The girls picked at the remaining food, though it had been sitting for quite some time. When it was clear they'd had their fill, everyone slid out of the booth and headed for the miniature golf attendant's window. Jay paid cash and the attendant handed the group five golf clubs, balls in different colors, a score card, and one miniature pencil.

"It's just the right size for you," Howard joked, pointing at the pencil. "The club might be a bit too long though."

"Nonsense, jerk-wad," Jay shot back. "You're just

jealous that mine is proportionately larger for my height.

"Woah, easy, boys," Violeta chimed in. "We're just talking about golf clubs here, I hope."

"You forgot the *miniature* part," Mac said. "That better describes these two."

"You wish." Larissa wrapped her arms around Howard. "Guess you don't know Howard as well as I do."

Howard grinned and kissed her. The others turned away in disgust.

"TMI," Violeta said. "Let's do what we came here to do."

They turned away from the booth and checked out the three courses. Families with younger kids clogged up the first two. Mac had been that age once upon a time, so he knew the parents would allow their little ones to putt a dozen times at every hole and spend ten times longer than a normal group. They chose the third course.

Mac was normally a decent putter, but this was not his night. The round started bad for him and continued to get worse with each hole, but everyone was laughing together and not bothering to keep track of the score. Jay in particular was chatty and loud, throwing off Mac's shot on more than one occasion to get laughs from the girls. By the twelfth hole, Jay had apparently realized that his best efforts had not gotten him any closer to

Violeta's affections, and he lost some of his comedic steam.

Mac was the last to putt on the thirteenth hole, a steep upward climb from the tee, then up a metal ramp constantly in motion. In the center of the ramp's top was a tunnel that led the ball straight out of a dragon's mouth into the hole, while the openings on either side of that one spit the ball out a few inches from the hole. Missing the rampart completely meant the ball would deposit out of the furthest exit from the hole or, worse, bounce back completely. Larissa, Violeta, and Jay all hit the hole-in-one effortlessly. Howard's ball entered the tunnel just to the right of it, but the ricochet off the low cement barrier was just the right angle to send it into the hole.

Mac set his ball down and got his hands into position around the putter's rubber grip. He watched the drawbridge rise and fall twice to gauge the timing. He took a deep breath in, pulled the putter back. He exhaled as he let the putter swing down toward the ball, but Violeta caught the corner of his eyes. His hands trembled just slightly enough to throw off the putter's path. The ball traveled up the incline at an angle, bounced off the concrete bumper, and rebounded back toward Mac. He reached down to grab it but underestimated its speed. The ball rolled down the sidewalk that led from the previous hole, went off course, and plummeted into the pond just below. His heart sank as the ball descended into the water with a loud plop.

"Just my luck," he muttered. He took one step off of the corrugated rubber teeing surface toward the pond when Violeta rushed past him.

"I'll grab it," she called to him. Mac felt his face flush hot with embarrassment. From the other side of the castle, Jay whooped loudly. Mac shook his head at the birthday boy and followed Violeta. Her putter was extended out into the pond. Just through the ripples from the spouting fountain in the center of the water feature, Mac could make out the pink ball Jay had handed to him before the start of the round.

"Can you reach it?"

"Hold my purse," Violeta said, shoving the small backpack she used to hold her wallet and other belongings at Mac. He complied, holding it slightly away from his body as if it were toxic or some offense to his budding masculinity.

Violeta used her free hand to hike up her pant legs, then took a step into the pond. It was slicker than she must have expected and her shoe skid across the slimy lining just under the surface. Without thinking, Mac tossed the purse and his putter onto the fake grass and lunged one leg forward, bending to grab hold of her. He too hadn't expected how slippery it would be, and his leg shot forward until he found himself nearly doing the splits. The water soaked up to his crotch, and its frigidness caused him to grunt with surprise. He reached out to her without thinking and Violeta flinched, lost her footing, and grabbed on to him. They both splashed down into the pond, completely drenched up to their shoulders, Mac on top of Violeta.

"Now that's what I call a great first date!" Jay yelled as the others cracked up uncontrollably from the edge of the pond. Everyone in the surrounding holes turned to watch the commotion, and laughs rang out from every direction.

"S—Sorry," Mac managed through chattering teeth.

"That first step is a doozy," Violeta said as she pushed Mac off her. She reached down and grabbed her putter. "Thanks for saving my purse, at least. Sorry I didn't find the ball."

Mac didn't know what came over him just then. As reserved and serious as he often was compared to his friends, the closeness to Violeta brought something out of him. "Don't worry, I'll grab it," he said, then dove in as if he were at the town swimming pool. He retrieved the ball right where he had seen it sink under the ripples of the fountain, then carried it up to shore. Violeta offered him her hand and led him out of the water. They both plopped down onto the turf and laughed as the other patrons went on with their rounds of golf.

"Oh gosh, my brother is in love," Larissa said. "I think I'm going to be sick."

Mac and Violeta both turned to her at the same time. "Shut up, Larissa," they said in unison.

"Are we finishing the course or are you guys just going to sit there?" Howard asked.

"Come get us when you finish the eighteenth hole," Violeta said.

"We need to dry off," Mac added. He saw the remaining trio of golfers resume play and turned to Violeta. "I'm sorry. All that for a stupid ball and we aren't even going to finish the round."

"Hey, that's the most fun I've had here in a couple years. Don't tell me you never wanted to swim in that pond when you were little."

"I guess dreams do come true," Mac said. "Though, maybe I should have grabbed some of the coins from the bottom while I was in there."

"'I'm taking them back. I'm taking them all back,'" she said in an impression of Corey Feldman from *The Goonies*.

"Best movie ever."

"Right?"

They sat there on the plastic grass, talking about their favorite quotes from the movie. Talk shifted to Feldman's other coming-of-age classic, *Stand By Me*, and other movies they admired. Despite their shivering from the soaked clothing, neither seemed to have any desire to get up and go inside until the others came back for them.

"It's laser tag time!" Jay shouted as he ran up to them. He slipped on a wet patch of turf and nearly slid into the pond himself when Violeta reached out and grabbed the tail of his shirt. "Why Violeta, you touched my bottom! Not on a first date, my love," he joked.

Violeta gave him a playful spanking and everyone laughed. "Dream on, birthday boy." She got to her feet while Howard gave Mac a hand.

The music blasted from the speakers in the laser tag arena, drowning out the bored employee as he went over the instructions and safety rules to all the awaiting players. Mac's receiver pack was strapped around his chest and back, pushing the frigid, damp clothing against him and making him shiver worse than when he was outside. The vibrations pulsed through the pack and gun as a timer counted down from ten, and then the doors opened to a cloud of dry ice illuminated pink and purple from the neon lights beyond.

"Go!" a robotic voice shouted as the countdown finished at zero, and the players rushed into the arena. Howard and Larissa had been split from them, teaming up with a group of seniors Mac recognized from school. A few middle schoolers were partnered with Jay, Violeta, and Mac on the opposite team. The team with the highest score after ten minutes—from points for hitting the most opponents' chest packs as well as targets in the opposing base—won the melee. The only prize was bragging rights, though there was an all-time leaderboard with 3-letter initials like SHT, FRT, and @$$.

After a few easy shots at the start of the round, each team traveled to their own bases to strategize, then scouts were sent out to find the targets, which moved before each round. Violeta and Mac were sent out as scouts for their team. The pounding beat of the techno song made it impossible to engage in small talk, which Mac was grateful for. Any verbal communication would have to be through yelling, which would give away their positions to the enemy.

They turned a couple dark corners, finding themselves at a tunnel just big enough to crawl through. Violeta gestured at the tunnel and shrugged. Mac gave her the thumbs up, and they crouched down. He waited for her to begin her journey through, but she waved him ahead instead. As he passed her, she brought her head close to his and called out, "I'm not going to let you stare. 'Into the garbage chute, flyboy!'" she yelled in an impression of Princess Leia. First *The Goonies*, now *Star Wars*? Mac was already crushing on her, but this sealed the deal. He hurried through the tunnel but found himself surrounded by enemies as he emerged on the other end.

Mac's chest pack vibrated and *blooped* as the lasers burst forth from Howard's and Larissa's guns.

"Gotcha, sucker," Larissa called out with a devious look, but her face fell as a beam of light struck her chest pack. Howard turned, but he was too slow. Violeta had zapped them both. There were ten seconds before their blasters would work again, so Mac and Violeta used the opportunity to run from their opponents. After a few more twists and turns around obstacles and catching a cluster of five seniors by surprise, Violeta pointed up at what looked like a neon glowing lotus flower about twelve feet off the ground.

"We made it!" she shouted and took aim. "'Don't cross the streams.'"

Mac understood the reference and played along. "'Why?'"

"'It would be bad.'" Violeta pulled the trigger.

Mac followed suit and with a few shots each, the lights in the arena flashed and the robotic voice announced their team as the winners of the round. Mac wasn't sure who made the move first, but they threw their arms around each other in celebration and their lips met. When their teammates crowded around them, Violeta pulled away and smirked before finishing the *Ghostbusters* reference. "'Total protonic reversal.'"

OUTSIDE, MAC'S EARS BUZZED FROM THE RIDICULOUS number of decibels the music had been pumping at. Violeta and Larissa had gone back to their car after the laser tag match without offering the boys a ride home. With the way Mac felt in that moment, he would walk home without complaint if he needed to, though he and his friends had their bikes locked up around the corner.

"The only thing that could have made my birthday more special would have been if one of the ladies kissed me instead of you dorks," Jay quipped from the other end of the bench.

"You'll find the right girl," Howard promised.

"You're too damn funny not to," Mac said. "Seriously, man, I don't know where you get your confidence."

"It's my good looks and natural charm. Maybe I'm just not meant for anyone in this town. I probably need to head out to Hollywood where the real babes are."

The ringing in Mac's ears started to get to him. "Why do they have that music so damn loud in the arena?"

"It has a hypnotizing effect," Howard said.

"Yeah, makes the ladies want to do insane things—like kiss Mac, apparently," Jay added.

"For real though," Howard went on, "it's like a magic show in there with the music and the flashing lights protruding through the darkness. Gets your blood pumping and your mind going all over the place."

Mac thought for a moment. "Bryan," he muttered.

"You kissed a beautiful woman tonight and all you can think about is Bryan?" Jay asked.

"No, fartknocker. I was just thinking, you know how Bryan told us when the stuff happens to him at night, there's a bright light that almost has a mass to it, and he can't move once it shines? What if there's something more to it? What if there's some kind of sound, a hypersonic frequency or whatever?"

"The kind only some animals can hear?" Howard asked.

"Something like that, yeah. What if it's such a

painful frequency that it causes his body to shut down so that he can't get up and run or fight back?"

"If he can't hear it, then maybe they can't control him," Howard said. "Brilliant."

"It was just a thought. I really have no idea, but I do know that we promised we would help him and we haven't done a single thing."

"But his dad is a psychopath," Jay said. "A literal felon. He'd probably murder us and chop us into pieces and feed them to his neighbor's cows."

"We still have to try." Mac looked at Howard and Jay and saw only fear on their faces. "Bryan is our best friend. Our brother."

Jay turned to Howard. "He kisses a woman one time and thinks it's made him a man, ready to go off to war."

Howard shrugged. "I'm with Mac. We have to do this."

"If I die before I've locked lips with some luscious babe, I'm going to kill you guys. However that would work." They laughed with Jay, then got off the bench.

"Wait," Mac said at the sound of a familiar voice. He pointed toward the shrubbery next to the sidewalk and climbed in, hiding behind prickly branches. Howard and Jay dove in alongside him.

Jason Unger walked up the sidewalk with two other boys from their class, Aaron Duran and Joey Filipski. While there was nobody higher on the great ladder of assholes than Jason, these two stood on the next highest rungs. Jason wasn't necessarily close friends with either of them, but they had a mutual understanding with each other that everyone else was below them. The only people they didn't bother bullying were each other. And, apparently, they liked to play miniature golf and arcade games together on Friday nights. A maroon Jeep pulled up to the curb, with Joey's brother at the wheel.

"Get in, losers," the driver said. Joey and Aaron climbed in, but Jason didn't join them. He shot a one-fingered salute at them, and they returned the gesture as the Jeep drove off. Jason stood there and watched as the Jeep exited the Galactic Dragon parking lot. An air of loneliness emanated from the brute like a wave of stench from a cow pie.

For a moment, a feeling of sorrow came over Mac. Next to him, Jay fidgeted. "Spider," he whispered. Mac slapped the little critter off Jay's arm and shushed his friend. Jason turned at the hint of a commotion in the bushes, and Mac was certain he spotted fear in the bully's expression, but after a moment, Jason shrugged it off and walked away. The boys stepped out of the bushes. Howard and Jay sauntered toward their bicycles, but Mac remained on the edge of the sidewalk. Even from a distance, under the glow of the parking lot lights, Mac watched as Jason looked up at the sky as if expecting to see something up there coming for him. By the time Jason disappeared, Howard and Jay had returned with their bikes.

"Are we doing this or what?" Howard asked.

"Yeah, are we dying on my birthday celebration night?" Jay added.

Mac turned to face them. "Whatever it takes to save Bryan." He pointed to Jay. "How much money do you have left over from your birthday?"

Jay counted on his fingers. "Including the money my uncles sent and the cash left from tonight, I have about a hundred and fifty bucks."

"I wish I had a family of doctors," Howard said.

"Wait, you're thinking about spending *my* money?"

"Whatever it takes to save Bryan," Mac repeated. "Now let's see if the gun shop is still open this late."

Chapter Seventeen
MAC

"You know, you really should have changed your clothes before all this," Jay said. Mac winced as his friend's elbow jammed into his ribs.

"Both of you," Howard said, gesturing toward Violeta in the driver's seat. He cowered as Violeta's eyes met his in the rearview mirror. "No offense, I mean."

The boys were crammed into the back seat of Violeta's family station wagon, with Larissa seated comfortably in the front passenger seat.

"My brother just always reeks," Larissa said.

"It's that slimy pond water." Mac pulled his shirt close to his nose and sniffed. The odor was somewhere between mildew and rotten eggs. "Smells like something died in it, though. Sorry guys."

"Turn left here," Howard directed Violeta.

"Besides," Mac went on, "if I stopped by my house

to get changed, there is no way my parents would let me go back out. They only let me go tonight because of Jay's birthday."

"You're very welcome," Jay said.

The car jumped the curb as Violeta turned into Howard's driveway too fast. Brakes squealing, the car came to a halt.

"Dude, why is it so dark?" Jay asked.

Howard reached for the handle and opened the door. "My parents are in the city for the weekend. Nobody home."

Mac noticed Larissa's head turn toward her boyfriend at that revelation. "Really?" she asked with intrigue. "Why didn't you tell me sooner?" Next to her, Violeta let out a groan of disgust. Larissa turned to her with annoyance on her face. "What? As if you haven't been romancing my little brother this evening."

"Mac, can you give me a hand?" Howard called back as he walked toward his garage door. He reached for the handle and pulled. The wooden door creaked on rusty hinges as it swung upward. Mac opened the car door and followed Howard into the garage.

It was quite clear from the first glance that Howard's parents didn't park their cars inside the garage. Boxes and crates and plastic bins stuffed to the brim filled every conceivable surface. They'd started on shelves, but soon sprawled out all over the floor and what had once been a handy workbench. A narrow maze wound around everything, leading from an old plastic

Christmas tree box to a bin filled with little league trophies to the *Ghostbusters* firehouse playset that the boys had played with until just a couple years prior. "I love that thing," Mac said, pointing to the toy. Howard glanced back, embarrassment flushing his face. *Toys aren't cool anymore when you're in high school*, his expression seemed to say, *especially not for guys who want girlfriends*.

Under the beams of Violeta's headlights, the boys made their way through the maze. "That's it." Howard pointed to an army green box that looked like an ammunitions crate straight out of a war movie. All manner of warnings graced the sides and lid of the box, pointing out the dangers of explosives, fire risks, not for use by children. Howard pulled up one corner of the lid, peered in, and nodded with approval.

"Grab that end," he said. Mac stretched one leg over a garbage bag bursting at the seams with old clothes. He grabbed the handle with both hands while Howard took the other side. At Howard's nod, they both lifted, but it was heavier than either boy expected.

"Jay," Mac called toward the car. "Are you going to give us a hand?"

Jay's head popped out of the right passenger window of the station wagon. "I'm good here. Someone has to keep the ladies entertained."

Howard tried to contain his laughter but failed. It came out as a snort. "Let him have his moment, I guess. We got this. On three."

Howard counted and both boys gave it another

attempt. This time, they hoisted the crate up and off its sagging shelf. Twice on their way out of the mess of a garage, Mac thought he was going to drop the crate on his foot as he lost his balance or stubbed his toe into various items they had to maneuver around. Jay finally exited the car as the duo approached the station wagon. He came around and opened the car's rear hatch for them, and Mac and Howard heaved the crate into the spacious interior, careful to avoid the ear protection and other gear they had picked up before calling Violeta for a ride.

"Are you hauling a dead body in that thing?" Violeta joked.

"That's my brother and his dorky friends you're talking about," Larissa said. "It's probably a huge crate of *G.I. Joe* dolls and all the little dress-up accessories."

"Action figures," Mac started, then stopped himself. He didn't want to turn into the nerdy little brother in front of Violeta, which is exactly what his sister was trying to make him do. "Just forget about it." He and Howard gave the crate a push to clear the edge. Mac slammed it shut and the boys crammed into the back seat once again.

"Where am I chauffeuring you boys to next? Jay's house?"

"Bryan's place," Mac said. "Please. We just need to turn the headlights off when we approach. You can drop us off at the side of the road before the crest so they can't hear the car. There's just enough room to turn the car around there so you can head back into town."

"Wait, you're not going to let us come?" Larissa asked.

"Bryan's dad is bad news," Jay said. "Better you let the men handle this job while you two relax—*oof!*" His patronizing was cut off as Howard backhanded his shoulder. "I didn't mean it in a sexist way," he whined, rubbing his shoulder.

"I don't like the idea of this," Larissa said. "My parents said Mr. Adams is a real creep. He might hurt you guys."

"Never thought I'd live to see the day you cared about my safety," Mac quipped.

"Not you, dork. I'm talking about Howard."

"We'll be okay," Howard said. "Promise. We aren't even going there to rescue Bryan from his dad."

"Then what are you doing?" Violeta asked.

The guys looked at each other, each hoping one of the others had a good excuse lined up. When nobody else spoke up, Mac sighed. "We just need to be there for him. That's all we can say."

And it *was* all they could say. If they'd mentioned extraterrestrials or UFOs or even rednecks in pickup trucks, the girls would think they were either lying or just plain crazy.

Neither Larissa nor Violeta pressed on his flimsy excuse. The rest of the drive went on in silence until Mac broke it. "Cut the headlights now," he ordered. A moment later, Violeta slowed the car to a halt. The brakes screeched and Mac's heart dropped. If Mr. Adams heard them, this would all be over before it started.

Mac opened his door and climbed out, with Jay following. On the other side, Howard exited and leaned into the front passenger window to give a kiss to his girlfriend. Mac found himself staring for a moment before he turned and headed to the back of the car.

"Wait," Violeta said in a stage whisper. She was out of the driver's seat and walking past Jay. Mac turned and watched her approach, but before he could react, she reached out with both hands, grabbed his t-shirt, and pulled him in for a kiss.

"How about one for the birthday boy?" Jay asked. It was enough to ruin the moment, but both Mac and Violeta cracked up. Violeta walked over and gave him a playful peck on the cheek.

"Take care of my man," she ordered him. She walked back to the driver's side door, reached in through the open window, and fumbled for something in her purse. She returned to Mac, who stood stunned from the kiss, and slipped a cylindrical object into his jeans pocket. "Just in case you need it for whatever you're doing," she whispered to him, then got back into the driver's seat. The guys pulled open the rear hatch door and retrieved their gear. The crate thudded on the gravel.

"Go easy with that," Howard whispered. "An explosion would do much more than just alert Bryan's dad.

"Sorry," Mac said. "Let's get this off the road." He closed the back hatch gently, patted the roof, and watched as Violeta pulled away and flipped the station wagon around in a three-point turn. She winked at Mac, then drove back toward town.

The boys stood there and watched the car fade from view, its rear red lights like the eyes of a demon, shrinking away until they disappeared. The only visible lights around them came from behind the thick, dusty curtains draped over the windows of the farmhouse.

"Are we really doing this?" Jay asked, his voice cracking. Without the girls around, he had no use for his tough-guy act. None of them did.

"Well, I ain't hauling this crate back to Howard's house, so we're really doing this." Mac tapped the box with the toe of his right foot and nodded at Howard. Howard nodded back and reached for the handle. The two of them lifted and made for the property. Jay gathered the rest of the items and followed closely behind.

Chapter Eighteen
BRYAN

I spent Tuesday working on the tractor with Dad. He had to go out to the supply shop to pick up parts to repair it with. By the time night fell, it still wasn't running. I couldn't possibly count the number of swear words that had come out of his mouth as we labored over the busted engine and the rusted frame of the old beast that Dad had inherited from his own father. It's not that the swearing bothered me on its own—I'd been through middle school after all—but it was more that it was directed at me, as if the condition of the tractor was my fault.

The words weren't the only things hurled at me, either. When Dad removed corroded nuts and bolts, he didn't just toss them aside, but lobbed them right at my face. The first time, a nut connected with my right eye. I swear that flecks of rust are still lodged in there three days later. When we couldn't see under the old lights in the barn any longer, we went back to the house. I made for my room straight away, but Dad had called me back.

"Where the hell you think you're escaping to?" he asked as my foot hit the first step. "Your mother made us a meal. Wash up down here and eat it up."

After we ate, Dad gestured for me to follow him to the living room. I reluctantly walked in after him and flinched as something flew at me. A cold glass bottle slammed into my forearms that blocked my face. It clanked to the carpet.

"You always been such a sissy?" Dad asked. I looked down to find what he'd thrown. A bottle of ice-cold beer sat at my feet. "Pick it up, dumbass."

I complied, crouching down and grasping the bottle. As I rose to my feet, something hit my shoulder and landed on the couch next to me. I picked up the bottle opener and popped the cap.

"I see you know how to open it. You been sneaking my brews?"

"No sir," I said with honesty. Back in the summer, Howard had snagged a six pack from his neighborhood's Independence Day block party and snuck it to Mac's during our sleepover the next night. Jay was the first to pop the top off one and take a big swig. That boy turned white as salt when he forced himself to swallow it, but being Jay, he of course had to pretend it was amazing. Mac and Howard followed suit, each taking a couple swallows of the beer, but when they all turned to me, I refused. From the moment those bottle caps came off, the stench reminded me of nothing but my piece of shit old man. I got up and slept on the couch downstairs.

"Boy, by your age, I'd already graduated to the harder stuff. You got some catching up to do. Take a sip, it won't hurt you." Dad's voice had a tinge of playfulness in it, and his face even hinted at a smile. I've seen how fast that can turn, so I wasn't about to set him off. I complied, putting the bottle to my lips. I took a deep breath, inhaling the sickening aromas that wafted from the narrow opening, worse than stale piss. I tilted the bottle, let the bubbly liquid fill my mouth. Nausea overcame me immediately, but I pushed it to the back of my mind and forced myself to swallow. Dad still eyed me expectantly, so I went on drinking until the entire bottle was empty. I took a deep breath and felt a rumble deep in my stomach. The room seemed to lurch for a moment before settling back to this shitty reality. I set the bottle down on the coffee table with a clink and belched loudly.

Dad jumped up out of his seat and pumped his fists in the air. "That's my fucking boy!" he yelled. The whole act was just like when he'd sit around on Sundays after the farmers' market and watch football, cheering for whichever team he'd sunk our savings into. "You hear that, woman?" he yelled to Mom in the kitchen where she was washing dishes. "My boy, not the postman's or the newspaper delivery boy's or the milkman's spilled seed, no ma'am. My own flesh and blood."

Without thinking, I lunged forward and grabbed the bottle by the neck. Dad's head snapped away from the entrance to the hallway and he met my eyes. I wanted to kill him. I wanted to break the bottle against the coffee table and use the jagged end to scoop out his rat-bastard eyes from his skull. We sat there frozen for a moment that felt like minutes, our eyes locked. He broke the stare, his gaze shifting to the bottle in my hand. A hint of rage flashed in those eyes, followed by a cruel grin.

"My boy indeed."

I dropped the bottle and ran off to my room. He made no attempt to hunt me down that night.

I WOKE UP WEDNESDAY MORNING SURPRISED TO STILL be alive. I got out of bed with the expectation that I wouldn't be allowed to go to school again. Why start the day with hopes I knew would only be shattered?

Dad looked surprised when I came to the breakfast table in my work clothes. By ten that morning, we had the tractor up and running. We worked through the early afternoon, skipping lunch, until the west field was cleared of the three years of weeds that stood taller than me. Dad hollered for Mom to bring us our meal before she had to leave for her shift at the diner. It would be her first shift since Dad's return, as her boss had given her unexpected time off yesterday due to Dad's release. Dad settled under the willow tree that was as old as the house and shaded our kitchen on hot summer days. I reluctantly joined him. We ate roast beef sandwiches and split a pitcher of iced tea that Mom had served us. Other than our chewing, there was silence between us. My gaze drifted off toward the road leading up to our long driveway.

"You expecting one of those boyfriends of yours to come frolicking up on a white horse to rescue you from me?" Dad asked.

"No, sir."

"I'm just messing around. Don't get your panties in a bunch." Dad belched loudly. "Did I tell you about the dude I nearly put in a coma back in lockup?"

My jaw dropped. "No, sir."

"'No, sir,'" he said in a high-pitched voice to mock me. "I'm not your damn drill sergeant, son. Anyways, this little dude was a real piece of work. Always kissing up to the guards, then snagging food off peoples' plates when the guards weren't looking. Snitching about any little offense. Just a real piece of work. About a week into my time there, I caught the fool alone in the showers. He was in the middle of shampooing his hair, eyes shut, so I just went for him, beating his head into the tiled walls, until he was out cold or pretending to be. I let go and he fell right to the floor in a pile of his own shampoo suds. I cranked the water as hot as it could go —and I mean scalding—and walked away. Everyone cheered me on, even the guards who couldn't stand how brown this guy's nose was."

I didn't know how to respond. My silence made him uncomfortable. He reached for his head and scratched. When he pulled his fingers away, a clump of hair stuck in his nails. He wiped it off on his grease-stained jeans without a glance. A beam of sunlight pierced through a gap in the tree's shadow, practically illuminating his head. A splotch of baldness shined in the light.

I reached up and scratched a similar spot on my own scalp.

By Thursday morning, the whole house felt like a pressure cooker ready to burst. Mom had brought home a Styrofoam container full of pancakes from the diner. When she mentioned that the breakfast cook, Hal, had whipped them up for her, Dad acted jealous and called Mom all kinds of shameful names I'd rather not repeat. I kept my head down and ate the cold, hard pancakes, avoiding eye contact with either of my parents.

Dad noticed a hair in between two pancakes as he sawed them to pieces with the edge of his fork.

"What the hell is this?" He held the hair up. It dangled, caked with flapjack crumbs and maple syrup. "Did Hal have you sprawled out on the griddle as he made these?" He flung the hair toward Mom, though it only dropped and disappeared on our filthy floor. "Sweep that up while we're out working. Make yourself useful for once."

The coward that I am, I kept my head down, though all I wanted to do was run over and hug my mother. She worked all night every night and slept very little in the day to keep us afloat. She didn't deserve being bullied by this asshole, nor did she deserve my cowardice. I took a deep breath, ready to defend her, when I noticed her giving me a subtle shake of her head. I let my breath out, pushed my plate away, and stood up.

"Time to get to work," I said and walked toward the front door. I grabbed the handle and turned back. Dad remained sitting, glaring at Mom. "You coming, Pops?" I asked. Dad stood up, letting his chair fall to the ground behind him, and followed me out the door without another word.

We had a late start to the season, but there was still time to get the cold weather crops sowed. We started with leaf lettuce, then moved on to onions and carrots. Mom brought lunch out when we were at the far end of the field, likely to avoid any contact with Dad, then went back inside to get what sleep she could before her next shift. All afternoon, Dad rambled on about his alleged prison antics, but all I could do was watch as he scratched away at his scalp, pulling hair off in clumps under his fingernails. By late afternoon, we'd made good headway on the rows we'd started.

"Can I go back to class tomorrow?" I asked Dad

once I'd worked up enough courage. He slammed his spade into the soil and looked at me like I was insane.

"You actually want to go back to that bullshit? You got a girlfriend there or something?"

"No girlfriend, sir, but yes I do want to go back."

"Some son of mine you are. More like your mother's kid. She's the brains of the operation. You must be smarter than you look." He watched me, waiting for a rise, and was angry when I didn't give it to him. "I'm only joking, boy. The answer is no, though. I need you here. Just one more week. Took us this long to get one field prepped and partially planted. We need seed in the ground by yesterday and we ain't even close. The winter chill is coming on quick. You want us to go broke and lose this place?"

"Mom has kept the bills paid so far." I don't know why I said it. I knew exactly how Dad would react. He pulled his shovel back out of the dirt and brandished it in both hands.

"The hell you say to me?" His arms trembled with the anger building inside of him. I looked at the shaking shovel, and his gaze followed. He released it and the shovel fell to the ground with a *thud*. After a couple seconds of silence, a twisted smile came over his face. "I think we both need a break. Let's cut it early for today. Get these tools cleaned up and put back in the barn. I'm going to hit the shower."

Better the shower than me, I suppose.

The day's events didn't end there, however. Mom

left for work at five that evening. She'd been in her bedroom with Dad for the past hour and came out with her face red from tears. She gave me a slight nod as I sat on the couch, flipping mindlessly through the four channels we got on our TV antenna. A half hour later, a pickup truck crunched over the gravel driveway and parked in front of our house. I opened the front door, not recognizing the vehicle. A man got out and slammed the door. He was short but wide and muscular. Beefy, like a pit bull, perhaps. Tattoos graced his arms—on full display due to the white tank top he wore—and up his neck. There was no doubt this was one of Dad's prison buddies.

"Is yer pappy home?" the man asked through a thick accent that sounded like it came from a lot further south than here. When I didn't answer, his face twisted to a sneer. "He never mentioned his boy was of the slow and stupid variety."

"Now, is that any way to speak to my flesh and blood?" Dad called out as he shoulder-checked me on his way to the door. He took two steps onto the porch, threw a beer bottle over to his friend, and turned back to me. "Don't wait up, shit-for-brains." He followed the guy to his truck, both men laughing at me. I shook my head and closed the door as they drove off toward town.

Mom and Dad arrived home together around eleven that night. This was wholly unexpected, as Mom's shift was supposed to go until early Friday morning. I stayed in my room with the door shut, but I had my ear to the wood, listening as they yelled at each other and banged things around. From what I could gather through all the screaming and crying, Dad had gone to the diner completely drunk and had made a fool of himself and Mom in front of her customers and coworkers. He had walked into the kitchen and found the cook, Hal, and proceeded to pick a fight with the man. The last detail I got was that Dad had threatened to stick the cook's hand in a deep fryer the next time the man flirted with Mom. Suffice to say, Mom was sent home for the night so she could get Dad out of there.

WHEN FRIDAY MORNING CAME AROUND, SOMETHING dawned on me. I had slept through the night the entire week and woken up in my bed, fully rested. No night visits. No lights. No bench on the porch. I reached up and rubbed the side of my head where the hair had been missing, but now I felt the spiky nubs of new hairs growing in. I was recovering.

Mom wasn't in the kitchen when I went downstairs. "Get yourself some cereal and then let's get at it," Dad said, and I complied. I poured a bowl of store-brand flakes and whole milk, then sat down and crunched away at it. On my fifth spoonful, I heard something from upstairs. Seeing the worry on my face, Dad spoke up. "Your mom isn't feeling too good today."

"She sick?" I asked, but I knew the answer.

"Something like that. Don't you worry about her. She had a bit of a fall down the stairs. You know how clumsy your mother is. She'll recover." The sound had grown more distinct. She was crying.

"Did she lose her job?" I asked.

"You kidding? That shitty diner would fall apart without her. Nah, she's going back this evening for her usual shift, don't you worry."

I was worried, though. I didn't know what kind of condition she'd be in. I didn't know how much makeup she would need to cover the bruises or the puffy eyes or swollen lip.

There was one thing I did know, however. I had to get rid of my father, and I had to do it soon if I ever wanted to see my friends and my school ever again.

By early that evening, Mom had come out, walked to her car, and driven away without a word to either of us. I watched her go from a distance, wanting nothing more than to run over and hug her and promise to avenge her, but I didn't. A damn coward.

Darkness descended upon us. After cleaning up the tools, we headed back inside. We heated up some Hungry Man dinners from the freezer, which I mostly enjoyed except for the chunk of ice in the middle of the mashed potatoes. The brownie never fully cooked in the middle, where the batter pooled like chocolate pudding, and the edges were burned and rubbery. I wanted to watch *TGIF*, but Dad said it was "for little girls," so we watched *MacGyver* reruns instead.

Now it's eleven o'clock. Dad is passed out on the couch after consuming another case of beer. I'm in my room and settled in for the night. After my earlier revelation that my sleep has been interruption-free all week, I don't have my usual reservations about the night.

And then the hint of a light shines through my window.

Chapter Nineteen
BRYAN

Out of instinct or perhaps habit, I freeze. Normally the beam of light comes at me and causes the paralysis. I can't fight it no matter how hard I try. But the light isn't of the same quality as usual. It's not even shining into my window at all anymore, though its distant glow still reaches my room, however faintly.

Did they change their minds? I scratch my head, running my fingertips along the rough patch where the hair is growing back. *Dad*, I think. *They're coming for him. They always have taken him, at least until he went to prison, and then I was the replacement.*

The revelation shocks me. All this time, I've been a patsy for him, a sacrifice. That asshole never deserved anyone to sacrifice anything for him. That leaves a bitter taste in my mouth. He takes and he takes and he never gives back to anyone. Just sucks the life from us like a vampire, siphoning anything that is good.

Let them take him, I think, and then I roll over, my back to the window, and fall asleep.

Chapter Twenty

MAC

"Put the flashlight down, butt-munch!" Howard said to Jay in a whisper that somehow hit as hard as a scream. Jay jumped in fright and dropped the light. It clanked to the barn loft floor.

"Up your butt and around the corner," Jay shot back.

"Can you guys please stop messing around and give me a hand?" Mac asked from the top of the stairs. He gestured for them to follow and descended the stairs where the chest waited on the barn floor. Mac took one handle while Howard and Jay crowded together at the other side.

"One. Two. Three." Mac counted, and they all lifted together. Mac walked backward up the stairs while the other two boys took most of the weight from the lower position.

"If you drop that, I'm going to kill you. I never even

got to kiss a girl," Jay said to Mac. "You both stole my two loves away from me."

The aging barn's stairs groaned with each step they ascended, but it somehow held up as they made it to the top landing and set the chest down.

"Let's check it out," Howard said. He unlatched all four bolts and lifted the lid. The hinges creaked, but Mac had no fear of being heard since the barn was far enough from the house, and Mr. Adams was most likely to be completely sauced or even passed out by this time of night.

"Freaking rad," Jay proclaimed. He reached in before Howard had even finished lifting the lid to its most upright position, but Howard swatted his hand away. "Ouch!"

"There's enough firepower here to burn down the barn, Bryan's house, and all the land it sits on," Mac reminded him.

"More like the entire damn town," Howard said. He looked like a kid proudly displaying his massive trophy collection. In this case, though, the trophies could make the night sky look like Camellia Flats was in the middle of World War Three. "Set all these off at once and they'll see it all the way in Raventree Hollow.

"Wooooah," Jay said in amazement. All three boys stared at the chest of fireworks, mesmerized at the possibilities and dangers of what lay before them. "Maybe I can just set one off behind the barn?"

"And wake up Bryan's dad?" Howard asked. "That

guy will literally murder us. There's no way he wouldn't hear the noise."

"Speaking of noise," Mac added, "we need to get the ear protection ready. If we don't have it on when they come, we'll be in stasis again while they take Bryan."

"If that's what really happens," Jay said.

"Mac's the smartest one here," Howard said. "If he says that's what happens, I believe him."

Mac smiled. "Thanks, dude. It really is just a hypothesis. And if it is specific frequencies that cause people to freeze up at their arrival, I still don't even know if what we bought will block it out completely."

"At least we'll look cool while the aliens probe us or whatever happens," Jay said, slipping on one of the heavy-duty pairs of over-the-ear protectors. "Space Shuttle One, this is Mission Control. You are clear to blast off," he practically yelled, unaware of his own volume.

"Keep it down a little," Howard reminded him.

Jay showed confusion on his face. "These work really good! I can't even hear your nagging."

Howard leapt forward and pulled them off Jay's head. "You need the other pieces first," he said. He reached into a bag and pulled out what looked like a large pill container. He unscrewed the cap and poured out two squishy foam ear plugs.

"Aw man, do I really need those? This works so good already."

"It's just in case that's not enough," Mac said. "I

don't want to be blamed if this goes wrong. At least we have twice the chances of blocking out the sound if we double up with those. It's just for a few hours."

The boys all grabbed their own double protection and looked at each other. "Do we have to wear them right now?" Howard asked. Both he and Jay looked to Mac, waiting for him to call the shots. Mac was reluctant to take on any type of leadership role; he much preferred Bryan or Howard to do that. Then again, this whole thing was about saving one of his best friends, and he wasn't about to let his own self-doubts get in the way of Bryan's well-being.

Mac led by example. He squeezed the foam ear plugs into shape and inserted them into his ear canal. He stretched the heavy duty over-the-ear protection meant for blocking out the booming shots of guns and slipped them on. The other two boys followed suit.

They proceeded to set out the various tools and contraptions they'd brought with them, then pulled three chairs into a half circle facing the window that looked out toward Bryan's house. Jay reached into his backpack and removed a silo-shaped stainless-steel thermos with a lid that doubled as a cup. He poured a steaming mug full of its contents and took a sip.

"Ah, nothing like taking my coffee black," he shouted, though Mac saw the grimace on the boy's face. He passed it to Howard, who took a sniff and winced with disgust. He passed it to Mac instead. Mac lifted it as if to say *cheers* and took two gulps faster than he should have. The coffee burned his tongue and the roof of his mouth. He handed it back to Howard in the middle of the trio, who finally relented and took a sip of his own.

"These are giving me a headache already," Howard said, pulling one side of the safety earmuffs up. "Can't we wait until they actually come?"

"Dude, we don't know when these things are going to show up. Better to feel uncomfortable for a little while than get caught off guard." Mac felt discomfort of his own coming on from the pressure, but he refused to remove them. He motioned for Howard to put his back in place.

Round and round they went for at least two more hours according to Mac's calculator watch, and even the discomfort and the cold draft in the barn and the throat-burning coffee couldn't keep the boys alert all night. Mac wasn't sure if it was Howard or Jay who dozed off first, but soon he watched them both fall into dreamland before he told himself he'd just rest his own eyes for a minute or two.

IT WASN'T AN OTHERWORLDLY LIGHT THAT WOKE MAC from a nightmare involving Jason Unger, stolen clothes from his gym locker, and being locked naked in the school's glass trophy case in the main hallway. Instead, there was a vibration so deep he could hear it rumbling his skull beneath the flesh, feel the shaking of the two silver crowns on his molars nearly loose in his mouth. The quality of the sound waves was no match for the protective earmuffs he and his friends wore.

Mac looked around, realizing then that he had the ability to move his head, then his limbs and torso. His friends had similarly drifted to sleep on the chairs on either side of him and woken up from this uncomfortable sensation.

"Feels like an epic fart from hell," Jay yelled to be heard above the vibrations and through the protection on their ears.

Mac faced the window, which was fogged up from the boys' heavy breathing. He leaned forward and wiped the condensation away and peered out. The night sky appeared cloudy, the light of the moon not quite breaking through but at least dimly illuminating the clouds from above. There was an unexpected quality to the clouds, Mac noticed. They moved quickly, though he thought it would take a heavier wind to cause such motion. In the sky just above the yard that stretched between the barn and the house, a split formed in the clouds.

"Did you guys just see that?" Howard asked, wiping the sleep from his eyes. Mac nodded, relieved he wasn't the only one witnessing the descent of what appeared to be a denser cloud where the normal ones had just parted. The new arrival was darker, not letting any moonlight pass through it the way the others had. It looked like a storm cloud, or like somebody's idea of a storm cloud that they roughly painted on a canvas using black and gray acrylics, not quite getting the multi-layered composition correct.

Nothing about this cloud looked natural.

"I mean, if you could see a gas cloud when you farted, that's how I'd imagine it," Jay said, attempting to mask his fear with humor.

"Shut up, dummy," Howard said.

The boys all got down to their knees, kneeling together at the window to get a better view. The object, that imposter cloud, continued its descent until it was nearly level with the roofline of the two-story house and the barn, spaced almost evenly between the two but favoring the house slightly. The vibration grew louder as it got to that position, then subsided into a steadier and more bearable thrum.

"The ship is lurking in that cloud. Keep your earmuffs on, guys," Mac reminded his friends.

Howard was the first to rise to his feet. "It's time," he said and walked across the loft to the open chest. He reached in and grabbed a Roman candle firework and one of the lighters. Jay followed and did the same. They both turned and looked back at Mac. "You coming?"

Mac took a deep breath and willed his legs to work, to get up off his knees and follow through with the plan to save their best friend from his near-nightly torment. His legs did not cooperate. He turned back out toward the *thing* that floated just outside of Bryan's bedroom window. He still had a good view of Bryan's window, where the room had only the faintest red glow from Bryan's alarm clock display. The intruders hadn't yet acted. "Maybe they know something is wrong," he suggested as an excuse not to move.

"Maybe they sense us here," Jay said. "Should we hide?"

"Cut the shit, Mac," Howard ordered. "You're poisoning yourself and Jay." He held the lighter in front of his face and flicked the wheel with his thumb, causing a tiny flame to spark into life. "Now let's do this. For Bryan."

"For Bryan," Jay echoed and activated his own lighter.

"Dude, no!" Mac jumped to his feet and lunged toward Jay, who held the firework in his left hand too close to the lighter in his right. The fuse only needed the faintest hint of fire to ignite. Sparks flew off as the distance to its base diminished.

"Oh crap! I didn't mean to!" Jay lobbed the firework into the air between himself and Mac. Mac had never been particularly athletic; his own father lamented his lack of hand-eye coordination on a regular basis, always reminding his son how disappointed he was that Mac never went out for the football or baseball teams. Despite all that, Mac swatted his arm out just in time to catch the airborne explosive. He pivoted as soon as his fingers wrapped around its base and dashed to the window. He pulled up the latch and pushed the two halves of the window outward. He took aim at the craft obscured by the cloud.

"Let's go, Jay," Howard called behind him. Mac turned his head to face them, his eyes squinting as he braced himself for the blast. He watched Jay retrieve another firework from the chest and follow Howard down the loft stairs. Mac's head snapped back at the cloud as a beam of light fired out of its dark form toward Bryan's window.

Thoom!

Everything moved in slow motion. A bright flash from the firework. A shock rippling through Mac's hand, up his arm. A high whistle sound as the firework shot out toward the cloud. Mac released what was left of the object in his hand, letting it fall to the ground below, and turned to watch the path of light. It zoomed through the air.

The cloud moved.

Mac had never seen a cloud take evasive maneuvers like that because that is not something a cloud can actually do. This one did just that, rising at an angle so rapidly that the shingles on Bryan's roof flapped under the strong current of air that hit it. As the firework passed it by, the craft in the cloud corrected course. Over-corrected, actually, bumping into the brick chimney that protruded from the roof. As it made contact, the cloud vanished.

There, just above his best friend's home, an actual spaceship hovered in the air. It was just as he had expected from all the episodes of *Unsolved Mysteries* he had watched, or *E.T.* and *Close Encounters of the Third Kind*. Yet it was different. It wasn't some miniature model brought to life by the power of movie magic. This was something he saw with his own eyes, a few hundred feet away.

The ship was like a disk, perfectly round yet angling wide toward the bulky middle section. It didn't appear to spin, yet the thrumming indicated something was moving like a helicopter propeller to keep it hovering in the air. Where Mac expected to see sleek and shiny silver metal on the exterior, the actual appearance was a greenish black like obsidian, glowing faintly. It wasn't smooth, either, but rather scaly like a reptile or a fish.

"Take this, mother—" Jay's voice was cut off by another blast. Mac looked down to see his friends standing just outside the barn door. Jay's firework shot off toward the ship, and Howard's followed almost immediately.

The ship bucked, narrowly avoiding the speeding flares. The boys hollered down below.

And then the ship changed course.

It darted through the air, right at the barn, skimming the roof. To Mac, it sounded like in a movie when the blades of a downed helicopter propellor or a boat engine are slicing through wood, getting closer to the fallen hero who must use all his strength to move out of the way just inches from losing his legs.

The hundred-year-old barn was hardy, but it hadn't

been built for an alien invasion. The shingles blew off and scattered like playing cards in a game of fifty-two card pickup. The wooden rafters split like twigs. Makeshift wiring that stretched across the beams from lights to outlets to more lights snapped and sparked.

"No no no!" Mac shouted as he watched some of those sparks fall straight into the open chest of fireworks. Mac didn't wait to find out what would happen next. He ran and leapt over the railing, barely holding on as his body dangled over the other side. He looked down to find the tractor just six feet below him. He let go, landing on the green machine with only slight pain shooting up his ankles.

Two pairs of hands grabbed him and pulled him down.

"We've got you, buddy," Howard said.

"Now we know who the next James Bond should be," Jay shouted. "Mac Alden, Action Hero!"

The boys ran out of the barn and halfway across the yard before an explosion blew them off their feet and sent them into the thorny patch of weeds of what was once a vegetable and herb garden.

"All those fireworks," Howard lamented.

"Your parents are so going to kill you," Jay said. "Dead man walking."

Mac looked up to see the ship hovering menacingly above them. It shifted and moved back toward the house. No longer wasting time, it sent another beam of light directly into Bryan's window.

"There's no glass," Mac said, squinting at the brilliance of the beam.

"What?" Jay followed his gaze. "How's that possible?"

Where Bryan's window normally was, the entire wall seemed to be missing. It was like some futuristic x-ray alternative that physically moved the outer flesh of the patient to see what was inside. From down below, the boys could see into their friend's room. They could see the edge of the bed, where Bryan slept, unaware of what was happening around him. Or, more likely, unable to move under whatever otherworldly power these beings had.

In moments, they were going to take him.

Chapter Twenty-One
BRYAN

The lights come for me once again. They must have had enough of my dad. They must have found him as much of a freaking disappointment as those of us on Earth. I could have saved them the trouble if only they'd asked me.

I lay in my bed, not able to move as that thick, milky light seeps in through the window, creeps toward me, envelops me. It's neither hot nor cold to the touch, not solid nor liquid nor gaseous. It reminds me of milk froth on the top of one of those fancy-ass cappuccinos you can get at the café at Raventree Mall.

The bedsheets stick to the sweat on my exposed legs and arms for just a second as I'm lifted; they nearly hitch a ride with me until they peel off and fall back to my mattress. A stinging smell hits my nostrils, metallic yet not like any metal known on earth. There is a choir of faint, high-pitched sounds like an orchestra of dog whistles, not meant for human ears and yet I can sense it in my head, in my sinus cavities, which swell and ache.

I'm halfway to the window, my feet ahead of me, hovering partly over all the crap strewn across my desk. Sweat forms at my pores and runs down my temple, into my ears. It itches but I can't use my arms to rub it away. My eyes feel dry, but I can't even blink them, like someone put a clamp in to keep them open for some twisted reason.

And then the explosion of a different light hits. It's multicolored. It has an immediate odor that I recognize from years of Fourth of July celebrations. It's nothing like the light that holds me captive. No, it is a light of this world, of this reality.

The beam holding me shudders under the firework's impact. I feel myself move through the air like when my friends and I would go to the playground and run around on the spinning contraption, get it going at a good clip, and dangle off the side as it twirls us into a gut-puking dizziness and all we can do is hang on and let our bodies flail in the air until it comes to a stop.

And then another firework explodes and the light's grip on me straight up disappears. My lower half slams against the desk but there is nothing stopping the rest of me from going down and crashing onto my hardwood floor. My landing is accompanied by a third pop outside.

"What the shit is going on up there?" Dad yells as he

comes out of a drunken coma on his recliner downstairs. "That you, boy?"

From where I lay crumpled on the floor, I can just make out the object in the sky outside of my window, It swerves, hits the roof, which rattles the house and sends books tumbling off my shelf.

"I'm coming in there," Dad slurs, now halfway up the stairs. "Your ass is grass!"

I take a deep breath and find my voice. "It's outside, Dad."

Another crash. I scramble to my feet and lean over the desk. I'm dizzy now. I must have slammed my head harder than I realized in the fall. Shaking it off, I look outside and see the cloud dissipating as the disk-shaped craft sails over the yard and the roof of the barn comes crashing down from the impact. My friends run out of the barn doors just before a massive explosion rocks all the acres that make up my family's farm. I stumble away from the window and open the door.

Light from the explosions still echoes through my vision, making the upstairs landing outside my bedroom impossible to see in the windowless darkness. I slam into Dad just as he finishes his climb up the stairs. In his inebriated state, his balance is nonexistent. He falls back without resistance and tumbles all the way down the fifteen steps to the first floor with nothing but grunts on his descent.

I run halfway down the steps and take in Dad's crumpled form on the floor below as my eyes recover and adjust. He's still as a stone. *I've killed him*, I think. *I'll end up in prison just like him.*

The front door opens a few feet behind him. Three silhouettes stand there, the forms panting, slightly hunched in pain from the explosion that flung them off their feet, but they don't seem to be seriously injured.

"Now that was some real action hero shit," Jay says.

"You guys came for me," I say. I take one step down and freeze.

The shadows of Jay, Howard, and Mac shoot inward and cover my dad as a brilliant light explodes to life behind them, and suddenly my vision fails me again. Before I can react, that unearthly light wraps its tendrils around my free will and clamps tight. Without the ability to fight back, it takes me away from my home.

Only this time, I am not alone.

Chapter Twenty-Two
MAC

Mac saw firsthand how the light Bryan had always described had worked its unearthly magic on him. It was more like a floating, glowing beam of milk with the thickness it had, but even that didn't accurately portray it. The slime that filled the sewers of New York City in *Ghostbusters 2*, perhaps, only more of a whitish color? When it hit, Bryan transformed into a statue on the stairs. Despite Jay, Howard, and Mac standing in the doorway, the beam traveled *through* them, not broken up into shadow by their forms; the only shadows came from their blocking of the lights of the ship itself. Its cosmic headlights, if you will.

Mac took satisfaction knowing the ear protection had worked. He stepped out of the way of the beam, into the foyer. Jay and Howard followed suit, stepping to the opposite side of the beam from Mac. They turned toward Bryan to see him lifted off his feet and pulled through the air in the path of the beam. At first the light moved him slowly, but as his body approached the doorway, he was pulled at a more rapid clip. Just as he passed the boys, they all acted on instinct, reaching out for their friend and grabbing hold of his clothing.

The velocity at which he was being pulled was too much for their collective strength. Instead of helping to rescue their friend, they were pulled along for the ride.

"Oh shiiiiiiiiiiiiiiiiiiit!" Jay shrieked. Howard and Mac screamed along with him, but neither boy was able to form any expletives to match Jay.

The wind slapped into Mac's face during the rapid journey into the maw of the ship. The light blinded as he approached it, and the boys were plunged into darkness.

The room surrounding them shuddered as the ship took off into the sky, away from Bryan's house. A pink glow sparked to life somewhere in the hold and rapidly dispersed around them. It was like a gas spreading, with millions of microscopic luminescent entities catching a ride on the cloud. Mac looked around and could not see any source of the glow other than the cloud itself.

A hissing sounded out from the walls around them as a hot liquid sprayed from unseen nozzles. Mac flinched and saw Jay and Howard doing the same. The substance was hot but didn't burn their flesh. It had a distinct antiseptic smell, like they were being sprayed by hand sanitizer. It reminded Mac of the hospital he'd spent a lot of time in during his grandmother's final days.

Mac took a step back and tripped over Bryan's body. He let out an involuntary *oof* as he landed, but the ground wasn't hard. It had some give to it, a squishiness like the waterbed his parents once had in their bedroom. Dizziness overtook him as the thought of seasickness came to his mind, like he was on a boat that never held still, always rocking under the waves of the ocean.

"Bryan," Howard said, apparently just realizing their friend was sprawled out behind him. He knelt and put a hand over Bryan's face. He turned to Mac, eyebrows raised. "He's breathing. Why isn't he moving? That light isn't on him anymore."

"Maybe it's a fear response," Jay suggested, reaching down to pull Mac up from where he fell. Mac took his hand and got back to his feet, though the wobbling sea-legs feeling hadn't left him. "Maybe his body just shuts down out of habit since he's been through this so many times."

"Where the hell are we, anyways?" Howard asked

"Some kind of holding cell, I guess." Mac said.

"Nah, it's an airlock," Jay said. "Haven't you guys seen any sci-fi movies? Spaceships always have airlocks, and they have to sanitize whatever enters to make sure they're not bringing in some kind of alien virus that will plague the ship's crew."

"Crew?" Howard asked, apparently just realizing the

ship must be piloted by something sentient, and probably staffed by others. "We didn't bring any weapons with us."

"Your fireworks all went up in that explosion." Jay used his hands to mimic the barn blowing up. "That's all we had." He and Howard turned to Mac. Mac felt his cheeks burn. He was, after all, the mastermind behind this operation, and it had failed.

"I'm sorry, guys. I really hadn't thought we'd even get this far. I thought we could scare them away from ever taking Bryan again. I never imagined we'd actually be taken along with him. I—"

"Shh," Howard commanded and held out a hand for everyone to be quiet and listen.

A groan of pain. The boys looked down at Bryan, but it hadn't come from him. There must have been another room next to theirs. The groan hadn't sounded inhuman.

"Who the hell is that?" Jay whispered. Mac stumbled toward the wall and observed for the first time that it looked like nothing he'd seen before. It wasn't made of wood or drywall or brick. He touched it, and his hand pushed inward like poking at flesh over a layer of fat. It had a wet, sticky feel as he rubbed his fingers along it. He put his forefinger to his thumb and pulled it away and grimaced as a snot-like string stretched and snapped apart. He ignored it and put his ear to the wall.

The groaning came again. "Stop," he heard in a

whimpering and groggy voice of a boy. "Please. Noooo..."

That voice. Even muffled through the walls, it sounded like someone he knew, but he couldn't place it.

"What's happening?" Howard asked. Mac pulled his ear from the wall to look at his friends, but it took some effort as the gooey substance on the wall stuck to his skin. Mac shrugged, then leaned back into the wall.

A thud. A scream. Then silence.

"Shitshitshitshitshitshit," Jay whispered rapidly.

A tickle in Mac's ear caused him to push away from the wall. He stumbled a couple steps away, but a string of the wall's slime stretched out. He reached up and pulled it off, but he had a feeling of something crawling into his ear canal. He rubbed his hands frantically on his pants and then stuck his pointer finger into his ear. It was wet as if he'd just popped his head out of the swimming pool, but he didn't feel anything solid.

He turned to his friends. Howard was sitting cross-legged on the floor. He had pulled Bryan's head up and rested it on his lap, rubbing the unconscious boy's cheeks.

Bryan's cheek twitched at Howard's touch.

"Shitshitshitshitshitshit," Jay continued in a panicked whisper. Mac walked over and put a hand on his shoulder to calm him, then pointed at Bryan. Jay's eyes followed.

Bryan sat up and looked around. "What?" He took in his surroundings and must have realized it was a place he'd been before. His eyes met Mac's, and Mac saw the fear in it. "No, you guys. You shouldn't have come. Now you'll be theirs too."

"No more leaving you behind, Bryan," Mac said. "If they want to fuck with you, they have to fuck with us too."

"Hell yeah," Jay said, his panic of ten seconds ago masked now by his pseudo-macho tone. "Ain't nobody messing with us when we're together."

Howard rose to his feet and pulled Bryan up. "Now how do we get out of here?"

"This is where they come for me when they're ready," Bryan said. "I usually can't remember it, but when I'm in here, it's all clear to me."

"There was another boy," Mac said. "He was screaming in pain or fear or both. Do you know who it is?"

"I never see anyone else here. I mean, nobody like us. Just... *them*." Bryan stumbled back, stepping on Howard's toe. Howard put up a hand to steady him and all four boys turned to a previously unseen door that had opened in the fleshy walls.

There, in the doorway, stood a figure that wasn't quite human, but close enough. It stood shorter than all of them; even Jay appeared to have a good three or four inches on it. Its head, larger than any of the boys', was strangely shaped and held abnormally huge eyes. They had a deep glassy purple tint to them, and it stared at the boys, cold and threatening. Its skin had a grayness to it, showing a faint pink network of veins underneath. Lines of wrinkles spiderwebbed across all the flesh. The nose was flat, even concave, reminding Mac of pictures of severe burn victims he'd seen. The being's lips were practically nonexistent, the mouth a thin, flat line, somewhere between indifference and annoyance. It wore no clothes, and Mac found his eyes falling toward its crotch, where a flabby stretch of skin dangled, perhaps covering any genitals like some biological act of decency.

"What... what... what..." The fear had returned to Jay as he struggled to form a sentence.

"Get him!" Howard shouted as he rushed at the newcomer. Without thinking, Mac did the same. He was already a few steps closer than Howard, but Howard's head start ensured the boys arrived at the creature together. They slammed into it simultaneously, knocking the surprised creature off balance and sending it flailing back and to the ground.

"Aaaahhhhh!" Jay yelled as he followed suit and ran forward. Pulling off a wrestling move Mac was sure he'd seen from Hulk Hogan, Jay leaped, then slammed down elbow first into one of the massive eyes. The alien cried out in a voice like nothing Mac had ever heard.

"Hyah," Howard grunted as he stomped a foot down on the creature's chest. A bone snapped within. The alien reached out a hand toward the nearest wall. Its fingers, twice the length of Mac's, with bulbous fingertips, dug into the stringy flesh of the wall. The pink tint of the wall illuminated at the touch, and the entire room closed in around them as the walls, floor, and ceiling expanded.

Jay bashed his elbow repeatedly into the creature's head. Howard kicked at its sides, shattering its ribs. Mac and Bryan both stood watching in shock.

"Guys," Mac finally managed. "The walls!"

"They're going to swallow you!" Bryan shouted. Mac saw him stepping toward the doorway to the corridor, but the door slammed shut with a sickly wet slurping sound. Bryan was cut off. A dull thud sounded against the closed door as Bryan slammed into it to get free.

Howard and Jay ceased their attack and looked around just as the pink fleshy walls fell in, encapsulating them into its mass, disappearing from Mac's view.

"Guys?" Mac called. Pressure formed all around him as the mass continued to expand and press into his body. His breathing sped up, but soon became painful as the surroundings pushed into his stomach, knocking the air from him.

He tried to move his arms and legs but felt total resistance all around.

His fingers... He could move them. He started with his pointer and middle fingers on each hand, scratching through the surrounding blob. He moved on to all his fingers, bending them into claws. With each movement, he felt the gelatinous mass shred into wet strings. His mind fell to the inside of a pumpkin being carved into a jack-o-lantern, those orangish-yellow, soggy, stringy guts inside. Soon he was able to move his hands, then his arms. He kicked his legs and felt the tearing. In one wide arc with his left hand, he smacked into something solid.

"Jay?" he asked. His voice sounded more frantic than he felt, a result of the decrease in pressure that had been on his chest, like he had just come up from a deep dive in the pool.

"Dude, in any other context, this would have been so freaking cool," Jay said.

"Have you guys seen Bryan?" Howard's question was muffled from somewhere behind walls of the gelatinous pink crap, but the substance was just translucent enough that Mac could make out his friend's form a few feet away, distorted, yet clearly Howard.

He wasn't alone.

The alien's form rose up next to Howard.

"Watch out!" Jay shouted, but it was too late. They watched as the creature's arms wrapped around the boy, one over his head and the other over both arms and his chest. The alien, an expert at navigating through the blubbery stuff, pulled Howard backward and seemed to swim away, out of view. Its arm over Howard's mouth muffled his shocked cry.

Chapter Twenty-Three
BRYAN

The entire consistency of the ship's interior changed into something I've never seen in my times here, at least not that I can remember. It must be a defense mechanism. I've always felt that the ship is alive somehow; these rooms are its organs and the walls its tissue and flesh. The moisture is its bile and saliva and blood. Those of us it takes are the food it consumes, shitting us back out into the world when it has taken what nutrients it can from us.

When the change happened, the walls that kept me in the airlock room changed with the rest of it. Suddenly there were no walls, no separate rooms. I can hear my friends screaming, calling for Howard. Something is wrong. The aliens have taken him. Through the stringy substance that surrounds me, I can just make out the silhouettes of who I assume are Mac and Jay.

They haven't realized I'm here. I aim to keep it that way, at least until I rescue Howard.

They came here to save me and they put their own lives in peril. Now it's my turn to rescue them.

I use the tightly packed contents of the ship to propel myself up and outward from the area that used to be the airlock. Instead of heading straight toward Mac and Jay, I take a longer way around them. After I struggle to travel what must be about twenty feet from where I started, a noise reaches my ears.

"Gggnnnuuuugggggh."

I hold still and turn my head to the right, sure that's where I heard it. I see a shape I can't quite make out. Something long, like a hospital bed? Someone is sprawled out on it, though I can't identify the bulk that towers over it just above what I think is the head of the bed. The figure laying down could be Howard; its head is too small to be one of the wretched creatures in control of this ship.

In case it's my buddy, I move toward him, pulling at the putrid pink strands and swimming through it. I'm perhaps ten feet away when everything rumbles. Like a spiderweb blowing in the wind, I feel myself swinging wildly. The mass thins out rapidly until it no longer holds my weight. I crash to the floor, which doesn't hurt as bad as it should since the ground is made of squishy flesh.

As the air clears, I look around and find myself enclosed by walls once again. I'm in a different room than where I started, and I'm not alone. I stand and look at the figure on the bed. His hands and feet are tied by veiny vines the same color as the rest of the interior. Machinery of some kind towers over him just behind his head. Another pink vine protrudes from the machinery and plunges into his mouth. I can't see how far it goes, but I imagine it snaking into the depths of his throat.

Is this what happens to me when they take me? Is that how I look, helpless and afraid? Do they intrude on my body's interior with that same serpentine device?

Without meaning to, I let out a small whimper. The boy's eyes shoot open at the sound. They move left, right, up, down, but he can't see me. Can't lift his head.

"Jason? Is that you?"

Gggwwrraaaawwrrgg is all I can make out from the sounds he makes. I walk across the room to him and our eyes meet. His face glistens in a jumble of tears, sweat, and the drool that excretes from his pried-open lips. The fear in his eyes turns to recognition. Desperation. Pleas for help.

I look him over. Jason Unger, the asshole who has made our lives a living hell ever since kindergarten. The idiot who defecated all over our belongings countless times, stole and destroyed Mac's bike just a few days ago, who had gone out of his way on a regular basis to make Howard and Jay feel subhuman with his constant barrage of racist insults. Here he is in nothing but his boxer shorts.

Let the aliens take him.

I turn from him and take three steps before his cries reach my ears again. I can't do it. I can't walk away from someone suffering under the same enemies that do this to me. I rush back. Without thinking, I reach for the appendage that has dug its way into his mouth and I pull.

Jason's bare chest protrudes. Beneath the pale, flabby skin, something takes shape. It looks like a snake. I pull at it, taking it out from the bully's depths, hand-over-hand, but it bucks in my grip. Its flesh secretes something wet and hot under my hands. My skin burns. The stench of whatever it released stings my nostrils, causes my eyes to water. Jason screams, though the sound is still muffled by the intruder in his mouth as I continue to pull at it. I must have yanked out four feet of it, yet there is still more. The writhing shape in his torso has moved up toward his chest, just between his ribs. Despite the pain in my hands, I keep pulling at it until the tip leaves Jason's mouth with a long strand of mucus. Jason turns his head away from me and vomits a mixture of puke and blood and pink slime.

I push the pink tentacle away. It swings outward, then comes back toward me. I look around and see a set of tools on a bedside table. I don't recognize them exactly as anything from my world, but one is clearly a sharpened cutting utensil, essentially a scalpel or a knife. I pick it up and lash out at the tentacle as it nears me. The tip slices off. Liquid sprays all around us, the drops sizzling as they land on my clothes. Jason screams in pain. I look down to see that some of the stuff has splashed onto his bare torso, leaving scorch marks like cigarette burns in a trail toward his belly button.

Using the scalpel, I slice open the serpentine holds on his arms and legs. I use my free hand to reach for one of his and pull him up to sitting position.

"Can you walk?" I ask. I half expect some kind of snide remark from him about being able to walk since I was still sucking on my mom's breasts, but he just nods. He slides his legs off the table and lowers himself. His knees buckle, but I use what strength I have to keep him from falling to the ground in his puddle of vomit.

"We're going to find a way out of this," I assure him, "but we have to save my friends first."

"What are you talking about? They're here?"

"They came for me. That's what friends do. Not that you'd know." I feel guilty as soon as I deliver the cheap blow.

I look around the room and see the shape of a door etched into the fleshy perimeter. I look for a way to open it, at first expecting to see some round bulbous hunk of metal like a regular earthly doorknob. I feel around it, rubbing my hands on the slimy surface, hoping for something.

"Move it or lose it, ass-wipe," Jason says. I turn just in time to see him charging like a bull. I dive out of the way just as he body-slams into the door and it flies open. He stumbles into the hallway and collapses to the ground.

"Sometimes being a brute pays off, I guess," I say as I step over his sprawled form and into the hallway.

"Oh hell no," a voice says from somewhere down the hall. I turn and see Jay, followed closely by Mac. Their eyes are on Jason.

"Of course," Mac says to him. "That morning I saw you stepping out of the woods, you were fleeing from wherever these bastards dropped you off."

Jason picks himself up off the ground and crosses his arms over his bare chest. "Anybody see my shirt?" he asks, looking back into the room he and I just came out of. It doesn't appear to be in there, and it's not in the hall. He shrugs it off and turns back to us as I embrace Mac and Jay. "Where's the fourth little asshole in your merry band of losers?"

Jay lets out an animalistic snarl and sprints toward Jason. I watch in surprise as my slight-framed friend slams what little weight he has into the oaf that is Jason, knocking the bully back down to the ground. "His name is Howard, fart-breath."

Jason lays there, stunned. He nods. "Howard it is. I'm sorry, Jay."

"What about Mac?" Jay asks, the rage strong in his voice. "You destroyed his bike on Monday. You torment him and the rest of us constantly. We never did anything to you."

Jason sits up and raises his hands in a placating

gesture. "You're right." he turns, his eyes meeting Mac's. "Please forgive me, Mac. All of you."

We all stand there, looking down at him with pity and disgust and hatred. Then Mac takes a few quick steps toward him. Jason flinches, ready for the blow he surely deserves from Mac's fist, but it doesn't come. Mac reaches out to him with an open hand, which Jason takes, and pulls him up to his feet. Jason towers over all of us. He's just who we need to win this fight against these extraterrestrial creeps.

Chapter Twenty-Four
MAC

"Where to next?" Mac asked Bryan.

"How the hell should I know?"

"You've only been here like a hundred times," Jay reminded him. His gaze shifted to Jason. "You too, I guess."

Mac heard the hint of uncertain fear in Jay's voice. Even though Jason had apologized, and even though they'd saved him in a time of need, Jay clearly didn't think it was safe to trust him. Jason had always been a wildcard. Even when he seemed to go years at a time without friends, he did all he could to alienate any potential allies. He'd just as soon throw Bryan or Jay or Mac to the aliens if it meant a clean escape for himself, Mac was sure of it. He also had half a foot and fifty pounds on Bryan, normally the biggest member of the group, so Mac knew that having Jason on their side for the next few minutes could be the difference between life and death.

Mac glanced up and down the corridor, its pink membrane walls reminding him of intestines pouring out of a character on a *Garbage Pail Kids* card. He listened as best he could to the sounds of the ship. A low mechanical whir vibrated throughout, but he didn't sense it coming from any particular direction. They had run out from his left, and Jason had been rescued from the room just behind him, and no noise escaped the door directly ahead of him. Mac turned to his right and started down the hall.

"This way," Mac said. Nobody argued. Bryan fell into step beside him as they crept through the corridor. Jay darted up on Mac's other side a moment later, likely still too afraid of Jason to walk alongside him in the back of the procession.

As they moved, Mac felt an itch in his ear. He slapped at it as if swatting at a pesky mosquito, but it didn't help. The feeling came from deeper in the ear canal. He used the tip of his right pinky to plunge in as much as he could, but it still didn't help. He felt moisture, pulled his finger away, and studied it. A stringy mucus substance dangled off, the color of the ship's walls. "What the hell?" he whispered to himself. He wiped the substance onto his shirt and tried to ignore it.

The tunnel curved to the left and ended in a door. "This has to be it," Jay whispered.

"Move," Jason ordered. The boys stepped aside just as the brute rushed forward and kicked the door in like a cop in a raid of a crack house. The door flew open at his attack, revealing what Mac assumed was the ship's bridge.

It looked nothing like the fancy control room in shows like *Star Trek*. Fleshy pink tentacles and off-white bony shapes protruded from walls and the ceiling. There were no windows, not even whatever the extraterrestrial versions of computer monitors were. Mac had no idea how the creatures controlling the ship knew where they were flying or how to land.

The answer, he guessed, probably had something to do with the two aliens who were held to the walls by tentacles, with those bony structures penetrating the sides of their heads where the ears would be on humans. *A direct link to the brain*, Mac thought.

The boys stepped into the room. To their right stood the being they'd fought a few minutes earlier, identifiable from the swelling purple bruises along his ribs and chest where they'd attacked it. It was pushing Howard against the wall as tentacles wrapped themselves around their friend like a giant anaconda preparing to suffocate its prey.

"Let go of him or die, bug-eyes," Jay ordered. His voice cracked, revealing the fear hidden beneath his tough little exterior. The alien stared at the boys, unsure what they would do. It took its hands off Howard, who slumped slightly before the tentacles caught hold and constricted, pulling him tight against the wall. His head hung with unconsciousness.

"What did you do to him?" Bryan asked. The alien cocked its head to one side like a dog showing curiosity. Mac shifted his gaze to the two aliens attached to the opposite wall—the pilots, he thought of them. Their heads trembled as if some electric charge was activating in them, but otherwise they didn't move themselves away from their positions.

"Let's kill it," Jason said and rushed at Howard's captor. The alien reacted quicker than the boys expected, turning to its right and grabbing hold of one of the tentacles that dangled from the ceiling like vines. It pointed the tip at the charging Jason and squeezed. A smattering of pink goo ejaculated from the tip and shot into Jason's face.

Jason dropped to his knees. "My eyes!" He fell onto his side, screaming.

"Shitshitshitshitshit," Jay cried. All three of the remaining friends backed up a step out of fear.

Mac's eyes met Bryan's, but he couldn't tell what his friend was thinking. Bryan reached into his pocket and pulled something out that glistened in the room's flesh-tinted light. He ran forward and lifted his arm. As he approached one of the two aliens fixed to the wall, his arm arced down in a slashing motion. To Mac's right, the alien with Howard made an odd sound somewhere between an insect's buzz and someone yelling *nnnoooo*.

Whatever Bryan had in his hand must have been

sharp. Mac flinched as the alien's blood squirted around the room. Each drop sizzled where it landed, including on Mac's left hand. He didn't have time to cry about the burning sensation, as the entire ship tilted to the left. Mac lost his balance and slammed into Jay. Both boys somersaulted through the air as the ship turned a full ninety degrees on its side. Jason fell from a farther distance and crushed both of them, though their positions quickly shifted as the ship turned fully upside-down and around and around.

After what must have been three or four flips, the ship stabilized. Mac heard rapid clicks and rings, perhaps some sort of warning sounds. He looked around to assess the damage. Howard had been anchored to the wall, so he appeared to be fine. His captor had used Howard's legs as handles to keep himself in place. Bryan lay at the feet of the alien he'd slashed at. The two pilots remained at their posts, though the one was bleeding significantly.

"Bl—bl—blood..." Jay murmured from the floor next to where Mac lay. Mac reached over and turned him onto his back.

"I don't see any blood, Jay. You're fine."

"No," he said, pointing to where Bryan remained on the ground. "Him."

Mac got to his feet and ran to Bryan. Sure enough, normal red human blood soaked through from the side of Bryan's belly into his shirt. Mac dropped to his knees and pulled the sharp scalpel protruding from Bryan's body and lifted his friend's shirt.

"Oh God, Bryan," Mac cried. "You—"

He stopped at the sight of a shadow to his right.

"Mac, watch out!" Jay screamed. Through his periphery, Mac saw the alien rushing at him with its long, bulbous fingers out like claws. Those fingers would not have been intimidating had they not been glowing with some kind of electrical charge.

"Aaaaahhhhh!" Jason yelled as he cut off the charging alien in its path and slammed against it. The alien responded by turning its sparking fingers at him and Jason's body lit up like a cartoon character getting electrocuted. The shock caused the massive teen to pop up into the air, bang against the ceiling, and slam back to the ground.

Mac got to his feet and backed up a couple steps until he reached the wall. The alien met his eyes. As large and dark as the alien's own eyes were, Mac noted a slight change in their shape. A glare, perhaps. A look of pure hatred. It lifted its fingers and curled them toward Mac again, taking one step in his direction, then another. Movement caught Mac's attention behind the alien as Jay sprinted across the room and pulled at the tentacles that held Howard captive.

The alien was three steps away from Mac. It let out a noise from its little mouth, some combination of ticks and buzzes. Just inside the little slit of lips, Mac could see a tongue fluttering around to form the sounds. A burning smell found its way to Mac's nostrils, stemming from the fingertips.

Mac's right hand brushed his pocket. Something protruded there. He fished it out, lifted his hand, and closed his eyes. He had never used one of these before. He didn't know if he was aiming it the right way, but he didn't have time to check. He pushed down on the top of the little aerosol canister with his pointer finger and heard its hiss.

"Gggnnnaaaaahhhhhhggg," the alien screamed. Mac opened one eye just enough to watch the alien bring its electrically charged fingers up to its face to wipe Violeta's pepper spray from its eyes and electrocute itself. The creatures left eye took the bulk of the shock, and the dark almond-shape bulb popped like a water balloon filled with swamp mud. The alien lost its balance as it stumbled backward, slamming into the previously untouched driver attached to the wall next to the one Bryan had attacked. The electricity transferred like bolts of lightning into the pilot, then snaked up through the tentacles that held it to the wall and protruded from its ear canal.

The ship bucked again. It turned and flipped and tumbled through the air. The buzzing alarms grew louder, and the interior transformed once more, popping open like airbags, the puffy, stringy, gooey material filling all the open space so rapidly that Mac couldn't make out where it all came from.

Seconds passed as Mac's stomach dropped and twisted like he was on the world's steepest roller coaster. It all ended in a crash into the earth, but Mac barely felt it, as the pink pumpkin-guts interior held him firm and secure.

Chapter Twenty-Five
BRYAN

I must have blacked out on impact. Maybe I just fainted from seeing the blood from my wound. That was stupid of me. Stabbed myself with the scalpel I'd stolen from these extraterrestrial bastards. I open my eyes and realize we're not in the air any longer. It's not just the change in the atmosphere—there was something about being up in the sky in this ship that had given a constant feeling of butterflies in my stomach and a lightheadedness. Maybe gravity was less effective when we were up there, I'm not sure. All I know is now that feeling is gone, and we're stationary at an odd angle. I must have rolled and flipped around as the ship tumbled to the ground because I'm curled in a fetal position several feet from where I last remembered being. I feel the blood soaking through my shirt.

"Bryan?" Howard asks in a groggy voice. I look over at him. He is slumped but still against the wall. The alien tentacles that held him taut are now dangling limply. He slips his arms out without effort, stumbles over to me, and drops down at my side. "What the hell happened to you? Are you okay?"

I rub my wound and hold my hand up to my face. It's covered in crimson. "You should have seen the other guy," I manage. "Seriously, I shanked the son of a bitch that was flying this thing."

"I... I know," Howard says. His eyes have a cloudiness in them like he's stuck in a psychedelic daze. He must feel me watching because he shakes his head like a dog getting up from a nap and meets my eyes, looking more like himself again. "Somehow I saw it all, but it wasn't from my own perspective." He turns and points to his former place of captivity. "It's like that thing plugged me into its system. I could feel the ship living, breathing. Feel its pain. As we tumbled through the air, I yelled at it to protect you guys, but I didn't make a sound. And then it did. That pink stuff..."

"Intergalactic airbags, I guess," I say. "Thanks for deploying them."

"Any time," Howard replies. He looks around and sees something he doesn't like. I turn to follow his gaze. "What the hell is Jason doing here?"

"That's who was screaming in the other room. He took some burning pink goo to the eyes trying to protect you."

From across the circular room, I hear someone shifting. I turn over and see Jay and Mac helping each other to their feet, grabbing hold of the dangling pink strings of this ship's guts to keep balance due to the angle it came to rest at. Mac looks around, spots me, and runs over.

"We gotta get you to a hospital, Bryan. This looks bad. Can you stand?"

I nod and climb to my feet, pretending not to feel the cold air finding its way into my insides through the nasty slit in my belly.

"Even if he can walk, I don't know what we're going to do about Jason," Jay says. He drops to his knees at Jason's sprawled-out body and shakes the boy. No movement. "There's no way I can carry him. The dude is twice my size."

"Let's just get outside and call for some help then," Howard says. He turns to me. "How do we get out of here?"

"I—" I start, but there's a crash and the whole ship shudders.

"There's more of them?" Jay asks. He leaps over Jason's body and crouches lower. My first thought is that he is trying to hide behind the oaf, use him as a human shield. When he digs his arms under Jason and tries to lift, however, I feel bad I even thought that. Jay is a tough one. All these guys are. They came for me.

"I'll check it out," Mac says. He walks to the door, which had slammed shut during one of the ship's tumbling free falls, and pulls it open. He disappears into the corridor. Thirty seconds pass. A minute.

"I should go check on him," Howard says and takes two steps toward the door before it swings back open. Mac stands there and I can't quite read his expression. He looks right at me.

"You're never going to believe this." He steps into the room, and two figures emerge behind him. Uncertainty overtakes me.

"The Valisellis?"

Chapter Twenty-Six
BRYAN

One of the Valiselli brothers steps into the room and takes in the sight of three incapacitated alien bodies and five kids, two of us seriously injured. His brother watches from the doorway. He locks eyes with me. My first instinct is to fear him, but I only see warmth in his eyes, and any fear bleeds out of me.

"We need to get you boys out of here before the reinforcements come," he says with a thick drawl.

"You really think we're going somewhere with you?" Mac asks. I'm shocked by his defiance. "You're in league with these things. We know you've taken Bryan several times before in your piece-of-shit truck."

"Yeah," Jay says, puffing his chest in his tough guy act. "We ain't going with you. I've seen *Deliverance*... Well, heard about it, anyways. I know what twisted things you intend to do to us."

"Jay," I say.

"What? My mom wouldn't let me watch it, but these hillbillies are all the same."

"Just shut up. Mr. Valiselli is trying to help us."

"Indeed we are," the older man says, holding his hands up in a placating stance. He's large, not quite obese, but has the figure of a man who drinks more beer than water and probably loads up on the butter and shortening when he makes a meal. His beard is long and curly, with clumps seemingly stuck together by grease and food particles. His light blue chambray shirt threatens to lose its buttons where his belly pushes it out. It's tucked into a pair of jeans at a waist adorned with a massive buckle. His boots appear to be snakeskin or something resembling it. His blond and gray hair is pulled into a ponytail, but several strands stick up in every which way. "My name is Waylon, by the way."

He takes another step into the bridge of the ship and eyes the carnage. Behind him, his brother leers in, a spitting image of Waylon sans the beard and some of the paunch.

"Nice to meet you, Waylon. You can call me Willie," Jay says. "I'm guessing your brother is named Kris?" Only silence greets him. "It was a joke. Waylon Jennings, Willie Nel—never mind."

"This one a comedian?" Waylon asks me as he steps around debris to get to Jason, still passed out on the floor.

"Name's Quentin," the other man says without a

hint of humor. He follows his brother halfway into the room. "You boys are lucky you survived that crash. We saw this thing falling from the sky. Ooh, nasty gash in your belly, boy." He reaches for my blood-soaked T-shirt and lifts it for a better look at my wound. "Let's get you to a hospital."

"Help me with the big one," Waylon says, and Quentin complies. They work together to lift Jason off the ground, each man wrapping one of his arms around their shoulders as Jason's feet drag. They navigate out of the bridge and through the corridors toward the other side of the ship. Howard looks at me with confusion but follows them with Jay at his tail.

I take a step in their direction, but stumble as pain shoots in every direction inside my torso. "Let me help you," Mac says, darting toward me. "They weren't kidding. You're going to need so many stitches."

Mac puts an arm around me, and we walk out of the room together.

"How bad does it hurt?" he asks me.

I wince. "I'd rather not think about it. What have you been up to these last few days?"

Mac gets that I'm trying to change the subject to get my mind off the fact that I might be bleeding out to my death right now. "Would you believe me if I said I think I have a girlfriend now?"

"Dude, of course. Any girl would have to be a complete moron to *not* like you. So, you and Howard already going on double dates with Violeta and Larissa?"

"If you count Jay tagging along as a double date. It was his own birthday, though."

"Shit, with everything going on at home this week, I totally forgot. Hope he's not mad at..."

Creeeeeeek!

I let my voice trail off as I stop in my tracks. I turn around, doing my best to ignore the explosion of pain as I pivot.

"You heard it too?" Mac whispers.

Clank!

"Move, move, move," I say. We walk as fast as I'm able. The noises sounded as if they came from an unexplored room somewhere back near the bridge. I hear more of them, getting closer, moving faster toward us than we are toward the exit. Up ahead, Howard and Jay and the Valisellis have already disappeared through a makeshift hole in the fuselage. Something squishes below my shoe and I slip, taking Mac down with me.

"Oof," I let out as I slam into the ground. I'm in a puddle of some sort. Sticky. Gooey.

"Aaah," Mac cries out. A slimy pink tentacle wraps around his ankle. I push through the pain and reach for it. It's warm under my grip and a layer of mucus-like fluid makes me wince. Mac kicks at it with his other foot and it recoils. "Go!" he shouts as we get to our feet. I look back and see a smear of blood where I fell. Maybe the wound really is as bad as they're all making it out to be. Maybe this is where I'll die.

As if he hears my thoughts, Mac says, "We'll be okay. It's just up ahead." I nod and push through the pain.

And then we hear the footsteps. Not just that, but noises coming from all around us. Slick, squishy, moist sounds. The pink membrane that lines the walls had gone a sickly gray after the crash, but now I swear it is regaining its color. "This ship is coming back to life."

We arrive at the jagged opening and look out. We're a good twenty feet above the ground, but the rim of the ship seemed to have cracked at an angle, making for what would have looked like a fun slide in more pleasant times. Mac helps me climb through the hole and we both sit on our asses, ready to slide down like we're at the local playground.

The pumping of a shotgun from down below beckons my attention. Waylon Valiselli's wife stands there, gun aimed in our direction, mullet poofing in the wind.

"Get the hell out of the way," she screams, and we comply. We thrust our bottoms forward and slide down to the dirt just as her gun goes off. A round explodes through the night air. As I hit the ground at the bottom of our descent, I turn my head back to see an alien staggering aimlessly for a couple steps and then falling, its head blown clean off from the shotgun blast.

Its lifeless corpse slides right for us.

Mac pulls me up and pushes me forward as the alien spews acidic blood from its neck stump like some twisted fountain. A trail of it follows down the slide, scorching the metallic siding. Mrs. Valiselli pumps the gun again and aims at the opening, but nothing is there.

"Get to the truck," she orders, but we stand behind her in shock. "Now, damn it!"

We comply. I take in the open tailgate and the scene on the truck's bed where Howard, Jay, and Waylon sit. Jason is sprawled out on a rough tarp that I've seen in what I thought were dreams. Mac helps me onto the bed and climbs up after me. Mrs. Valiselli slams the tailgate shut and runs to the passenger side of the cab. Quentin is behind the wheel, gunning the engine, and we speed away. The truck's suspension screams, waking up any wildlife in the vicinity. I look back at the ship crashed into the field and smile, knowing that it's not going to be airborne anytime soon.

Unless it truly is alive.

Unless it can heal itself.

"Faster, damn it!" Waylon calls into the cab through the open rear window.

"The boys will be fine," his wife calls back.

"It ain't the boys I'm worried about, Darcy." He turns away from his wife and looks back the way we've just come from. His eyes widen into saucers. I follow his gaze.

"Oh shit..."

Chapter Twenty-Seven
MAC

Mac looked down at Jason and wondered how they all got there. Life was strange, its mysteries beyond his comprehension. Even science hadn't brought humans to a full understanding of the world around them. The *galaxy* around them, more like. Science hadn't prepared them for anything they had come across tonight. Actual freaking aliens. An intergalactic spaceship that was also somehow alive inside. And especially the weirdest element of all: Jason Unger, apparently on their side and relying on his most frequent victims to save him.

Jason stirred and his eyes opened, strings of the pink goo stretching across his eyelids. Mac wondered if this was not the first time he'd awoken late at night or early in the morning in the back of this very truck, if the Valisellis had rescued him as often as they had Bryan. From the shock on his face, Mac thought maybe it really was the first time. Then he realized why Jason looked so terrified as the larger boy reached down to feel his pants. Mac's eyes followed Jason's hands to the boy's crotch, soaked through with piss. He looked away quickly, not caring about adding to Jason's embarrassment as much as not wanting to add one more reason for the cretin to attack him at school.

The commotion from Waylon Valiselli was enough to distract him from reveling in the bully's sudden misfortune.

"Damn it! How is it possible?" Waylon shouted out to nobody in particular. "That ship was in shambles. The pilots looked dead to me."

Mac followed his gaze. Up in the sky, rising from the crash site, the ship took flight once again.

"Just stop panicking and stick to the plan," Darcy Valiselli called back from the truck's cab. She reached her arm through the back sliding window and pounded on the metal tool chest affixed to the truck bed. "You know what to do."

Waylon nodded, then crawled from the rear of the bed, past Jay and Howard. The truck bounced over the rough terrain, sending Mac and his friends flying a few inches off the surface of the bed and slamming back down, yet Waylon seemed so used to operating under the commotion that he wasn't fazed in the least. He unclasped the latches on the tool chest and pulled the lid open.

"What the hell is that?" Jay asked as Waylon brought out a photography tripod and handed it to him.

"Exactly what it looks like, so get those legs out and locked and hold on to it," Waylon ordered. Jay complied while Waylon fished around in the chest for more strange items. The next object he pulled out was a saucer shape with a cone sticking out in the center of the dip. It reminded Mac of a much smaller version of the satellite dishes some of the more remote farmhouses around town used to pick up television stations since the cable company didn't service their area.

Jay kept his grip on the tripod as Waylon affixed the dish to it. The wind pushed at the contraption as the truck sped through the dirt roads, but Jay held firm. Waylon next retrieved what looked like a road case from a touring band of musicians. It thudded onto the bed and Waylon undid two clasps on either side of its front face and removed the casing. Inside were rack-mounted electronics. Sound equipment, something Mac would expect to see in pictures of concert stages or recording studios. A tangle of wires dangled below the interfaces. Waylon reached in and grabbed two, securing the ends into the back of the satellite dish.

"They're getting closer," Howard called. He had moved to comfort Bryan, who was hunched over in pain from his wounds. Mac felt helpless as he sat next to his tormentor.

"Not for long," Waylon said. He fiddled with some

knobs on the interface. "What the hell?" he grunted as nothing appeared to happen. "Why isn't it working?"

Mac looked to the sky behind them. The ship was indeed getting closer. It was near enough that he could see the area that had been busted through, where they were able to exit the ship after the crash. The jagged shape of the hole was still visible, but a pink membrane had formed over it, keeping the cold, late night air out of the ship's interior. Other spots on the ship's perimeter should have appeared more damaged after the crash, but it had apparently been able to heal itself. It was truly alive.

"What are we going to do?" Jay asked. "Send it some bad movies and hope to distract it?"

"Shut the hell up, kid," Waylon yelled and then turned toward the cab. "Why isn't it working?" he asked his brother and wife.

"Power, you dolt." Quentin called back. He reached his hand through the cab's back window. "Give me the power cable."

Waylon fumbled with the tangle of cables in the road case and pulled one out that had been haphazardly soldered to a cigarette lighter plug. He handed it to Quentin, who pulled it into the cab. Mac turned back to the ship. It was gaining on them quickly, the heat of its glow warming his skin.

He remembered something.

"We lost our earmuffs!" Mac shouted to his friends.

"We'll be useless without them when it sends its beam to us!"

"They're the ones that are going to need hearing protection," Waylon said with a twisted smile. He flicked a switch on one of the interfaces, turned a knob, and reached for the satellite dish on the tripod that Jay still held a firm grasp on. "Need to adjust this," he said to Jay, who just nodded and continued looking confused. Waylon pivoted the satellite so that the center cone pointed right at the pursuing ship. "Keep it aimed there."

Waylon continued to fiddle with the knobs and switches. A series of multicolored lighted meters on one of the interfaces in the case spiked upward, from green to yellow to red. Mac had seen documentaries about bands in the studios, had played with his dad's stereo enough to know that red meant *way too freaking loud for this thing to handle*, and yet he heard nothing.

"Why isn't it working?" Mac asked. Waylon flashed him a devious smile.

"Oh, it's working alright, we just can't hear this frequency." He pointed to the ship. "But they can."

Mac followed his gaze. The ship was still behind them but moving erratically. It swerved off to the left. The right. Dipped, but corrected course.

"How about just a little more juice," Waylon said, and cranked a knob to eleven.

The ship pivoted hard to its right, then nosedived straight down to the earth. The impact rumbled the ground. Mac had never been to California, had never experienced an earthquake like the one that interrupted the World Series a couple years ago, but he imagined this is what it felt like. The truck buckled over the shifting ground, swerving, clipping a tree, and bouncing back the opposite direction. Mac was knocked off his knees and fell onto Jason, wincing as his hand brushed the bully's piss-soaked crotch. Howard held firm to Bryan, who grunted in pain.

"Ballsacks!" Jay shouted as he lost his grasp on the tripod. Top-heavy, it tilted right over the edge of the truck bed and plummeted to the ground.

"It did its job," Waylon reassured him. "Fried itself, too, most likely. I don't think those alien bastards are going to mess with you boys again any time soon. They better hope they have a good mechanic onboard after that crash."

The truck sped along, no longer pursued by an otherworldly aerial craft, but things weren't over yet. "We need to get Bryan to a hospital," Howard said. "This looks really bad." He had Bryan's shirt pulled up. From across the truck bed, Mac thought he could see Bryan's guts in the mess of blood. After everything they'd gone through that night, it couldn't end like this, Mac thought. It couldn't end with Bryan dying from his own accidental stab wound. Yet there was absolutely nothing that Mac could do.

He reached up to his ear. It felt itchy. Tingly. He couldn't get his finger in far enough to reach where it bothered him most. He wished he had a cotton swab to poke at it. The tingle shifted, moved beyond his ear canal. Mac rubbed at the scalp over his temple and pulled his fingers away. He looked at them. They were covered in hair.

Chapter Twenty-Eight
BRYAN

The truck jumps one more time as it leaves the dirt path for an actual paved road. That last bump sends bolts of pain through my midsection like lightning. Maybe it's what Jason felt when he was electrocuted by those monsters on the ship earlier. I look over to him, still sprawled out on that tarp I know too well. He seems worse off than I am even though he's not bleeding. Maybe he's just being a baby though. I wouldn't put it past him.

"We'll be there soon, dude," Howard says. I'm laying with my head on his lap. The one person who would never let me hear the end of it is Jason, and he's two feet away from me, but I've already seen what kind of condition he's in, piss and all. He's not going to care right now. "Just hang in there."

"Who the hell is this?" Waylon asks. I lift my head slightly to see him at the front of the truck bed. He looks over me, behind us, as if we're being pursued by something. *The aliens are back!*

I force myself into a slumped sitting position and look back and up, but nothing is in the sky. Then my gaze lowers to the road behind us. The highway is only one lane in each direction, but there are two sets of headlights side by side coming our way. Two vehicles clogging the road with no worries about any cars coming in the opposite direction. It's the middle of the night or early morning at best, still well before dawn, so it's not like there is going to be any commuter traffic cruising down the highway. It's just us and them, and they're gaining on us quickly.

Their horns blare as they approach. Through the beams of their headlights, I can make out the vehicles. Two pickup trucks, raised high. Our town is small enough that trucks like these stand out. Billy John Garnsey and Murphy Neale are the drivers, a couple of good-ol' boys, which is a nicer term for boisterous and racist drunken redneck schmucks, traitorous Confederate flags flying high from their trucks. As they get closer, I hear them and other trashy members of their crew hooting and hollering as they speed our way.

"Get down, boys," Waylon orders, and suddenly I realize his fear. The Valisellis are known as complete weirdos in our town, and no respectable parents would let their kids ride around with them in daylight, let alone in the middle of the night. Especially kids that are bleeding and battered. It's not that the opinions of Billy

John, Murphy, and their ilk matter all that much, but it still would not look good.

Murphy's truck speeds past us in the wrong lane on the left while Billy John lays on the horn and flashes his high beams at us. His pickup gets so close that the front end practically towers over the back edge of the Valisellis' truck bed. I can feel the heat of the engine only a couple feet from my face. Finally, he swerves off to the left and follows his buddy.

"Woooo! Feel my wrath, bitches," Billy John shouts and laughs boisterously. He holds up a can of light beer and smashes it against his forehead as he passes. He's so laughably cartoonish that I can't help but shake my head. That seems to be when he takes in the odd ensemble in our truck.

Billy John speeds ahead, then swerves partway into our lane and slams on his brakes. Quentin is blessedly at full attention and reacts quickly, though all he can really do is slam on his own brakes. Hard. As the tires screech, the truck rocks and swerves. Waylon was on his knees and his body pounds the hardest against the cab of the truck. Jason rolls and pins Mac against the driver's side wall of the bed and Jay tumbles toward them. Howard holds me and somehow keeps us from flying across the bed or flinging to our deaths. The Valisellis' truck stops six feet from impact with Billy John's.

"Ahh!" Darcy screams from inside the cab as her face slams into the dashboard. "Son of a bitch!" The truck at a standstill, she opens the door and jumps out. It's not graceful. Her head must be spinning from the impact as she stumbles and falls over into the gravel at the side of the road. Quentin opens his door and steps out onto more stable footing. He reaches behind his seat and comes out with the shotgun that Darcy had used to blast that alien's head off at the crash site. By the time he brings the gun into position, it's too late.

"Cute toy there," Billy John calls. He's standing outside his truck, somehow already around to the passenger side. He has a hunting rifle aimed at Quentin. I'd put my bet on Quentin with a shotgun if that was all he was up against, but three of Billy John's friends in the bed of his truck are also standing with guns of their own, two aimed at Quentin and one at Darcy as she struggles back into standing position. Quentin sets the shotgun down on the concrete, kicks it a few feet in front of him, and takes a step back. Billy John closes in the distance and reaches for it. Beyond his truck, Murphy's truck makes a U-turn and pulls up on the other side. His is also full of their crew, armed and drunk and stupid.

"We was just out hunting when we stumbled upon this very strange little scene," Billy John goes on. "Imagine my surprise seeing you three freaks. Now, we all know you like to *keep it in the family*, so what in the hell would you be doing in the middle of the night with a bunch of teens from town way out here on a remote highway? I think the reward for catching a kidnapper must be, what, like ten thousand dollars per head?" He turns back to his friends. "We're going to be rich, boys!"

"We ain't kidnapped nobody," Waylon says as he climbs down the side of the truck bed to the road behind Quentin. He holds his hands up to show he is unarmed. "We rescued these kids and we're on our way back into town. Two of them need a hospital, and you're preventing them from getting there safely."

"Rescue from what?" Murphy asks as he comes alongside Billy John. "I say we let the cops decide that one." He jogs to Billy John's passenger-side door and opens it. He fumbles with something inside and turns to face us again. "I'm calling the dispatcher from the CB radio."

As Murphy talks with someone on the other end, Jay jumps up. "Listen you penis wrinkles, we need to get our buddies to the hospital right fucking now, so get the hell out of our way before we run you down where you stand!"

"I—" Billy John begins, but he doesn't know what to say. He looks to his gang, but nobody offers solutions. "Just sit down and shut up, boy. The police will help you as soon as they get here."

"Five minutes," Murphy says, throwing the radio receiver back into the cab.

The pain in my stomach forces me back down, my face pressed into the gritty filth of the truck bed, and I black out.

Chapter Twenty-Nine
BRYAN

The light is blinding but I don't panic. It doesn't have the quality of the beam from that ship. It's not the headlights of two rednecks' trucks. Nor is it even the sun. It's a sterile kind of light found in a dentist's office, or more likely a hospital.

As my consciousness comes back to me, I hear commotion in the room. Whispers turn to excited proclamations.

"He's waking up!" Jay calls out.

"Shh," Howard shushes. "Let him keep sleeping."

"He's already awake, turd-breath."

Mac's face is the first I see. He stands to my right. Violeta is behind him, her hands on his shoulders. Howard, Larissa, and Jay come up next to them.

"Honey, you're okay." I turn to my left. Mom is walking into the room. She has her waitress uniform on.

She must have been called at the diner near the end of her shift. Her eyes are red from crying and still puffy from Dad's anger. She looks ten years older than when Dad first came back from jail. I hate myself for even being a small piece of the stress put on her this week.

"Mom," I say as I reach toward her. I wince at the pain in my torso. Something feels tight. It stings.

"They gave you a lot of stitches," she explains. "The doctor said it was a miracle that no arteries were hit, nothing was seriously punctured. They had to clean you up to prevent any infection and then stitch you up. Your clothes were ruined."

"Did you go home?" I ask. My voice comes out scratchy from the dryness in my throat. "Dad..."

"He's here too, honey."

In a panic, I look around. My friends are still here, but nobody else. "Where?"

"Don't worry, you're safe from him. He's under police watch in another room. It seems he decided to burn down the barn in a drunken rage and then tried to go upstairs to sleep it off. The fire brought the emergency services, and they found him at the bottom of the stairs where he'd landed after falling all the way down."

My eyes meet hers, and I feel like something else is there. A knowing look, as if she suspects I shoved him down the stairs and she's okay with it. Thankful, even.

"He's not coming back home. Having the police around, seeing you in pain, it was an easy choice. I told them how he's treated us since his return. It's a violation of his parole. He may have squandered his second chance, but he's not getting a third. It's just going to be you and me, Leslie."

I smile at her with pride. A joy I haven't felt in days washes over me, lifts my spirits. I turn toward my friends. "What happened to the Valisellis?" I ask.

Jay lights up. "Dude, after I stood up to Murphy and Billy John and their dumbass group, they were all kinds of flustered. The cops came and cited them for having unlicensed guns, but they also took the Valisellis."

"I think they'll get out," Howard says. "I gave a statement."

"We all did," Mac adds. "Told them everything."

"Everything?" I ask.

Jay pats my foot. "They think we're completely nuts, but we told them about the ship, the creatures inside it, everything."

"I don't know if it helped the Valisellis' case," Mac says. "Lieutenant Friedman said it sounds like the Valisellis brainwashed us, told us to say those things to take the blame off them."

"You guys do sound insane," Larissa chimes in. "Mom's never going to let you out of the house again, Mackenzie."

"I think we can help them, though," Mac says. "We just need to prove what happened. I tried explaining to the cops where the ship crashed, but they wouldn't hear it. I asked them to bring me a map and I could point out approximately where the ship crashed both times, but they sent me away instead."

I notice something different about Mac's appearance. I reach for his head. He flinches out of instinct and then remembers it's just me. I touch a patch on the side of his head. "What happened here?"

Mac rubs the spot and looks flustered. "It's nothing. Think I just burned it in that ship or something." He's my best friend, though. I know when he's lying. I don't push it right now, but I know I'll have to talk to him about it eventually.

A nurse comes in and breaks up the reunion. She tells everyone I need my rest. I take one last look at everyone before they leave the room. All three of the guys are battered and bruised, but they'll be okay. Howard and Larissa are holding hands. Violeta hovers close to Mac, and it's clear to me they're an item now. Jay is, well, Jay. Mom is confused by everything, but I know she's going to be so much better off now knowing that Dad is not going to hurt her again. I say goodbye to them and let the nurse change my bandages. The painkillers she gives me send me back into a deep sleep. I have nothing but good dreams.

Chapter Thirty
MAC

Mac left the hospital after spending his second straight day visiting Bryan. They'd played games at Bryan's bedside table, he'd snuck in junk food for his friend, and mostly they had just chatted. He had told Bryan all about what happened between him and Violeta during Jay's birthday celebration. Bryan was excited for him. Mac even spent a couple hours visiting Jason Unger, who acted standoffish at first, but warmed up to his presence quickly. They watched a movie together on the TV in Jason's room since they didn't have much to say to each other, but Jason needed the company. There were no friends coming to visit him, just Mr. Unger and Mac.

It was evening, and Violeta had her headlights on as her car idled outside at the curb. "Thanks for picking me up," Mac said when he buckled his seatbelt.

"Hope you're not in too much of a hurry to get

home," she said. "Larissa said your parents drove into the city for a date night, so they won't care if you're out late. I thought we could park somewhere remote. Spend some time alone."

Mac smiled. "That sounds perfect."

Violeta drove out of town on the same highway where Mac and his friends had had an eventful night just a couple days prior. It was about twenty minutes down the road to the Crest, a popular lookout point over the valley and a spot Mac had heard teenage couples went to make out or whatever else. Fifteen minutes into the drive, though, Mac noticed a familiar turnout.

"Make a left up ahead," he said, pointing to the spot. Violeta pushed down on the brakes and brought the car near a halt. She made a turn onto the dirt road, and her station wagon bounced on the uneven terrain.

"Are you sure about this?" she asked. "I mean, I know I said remote, but this is like next level."

"I just need to see something."

"The crash site? Are you sure it's safe?"

"We'll find out." As they drove on, they passed the remains of the satellite dish and tripod that had launched off the back of the Valisellis' truck. "Not far now."

A minute later, she brought the car to a stop over what was clearly the impact site. A huge ditch roughly saucer-shaped spread out before them. The ground was charred as if a fire had broken out. Cracks in the earth spiderwebbed outward from the center in every direction.

"No wreckage," Mac said as he opened the door and stepped out of the car. Violeta left the headlights on as she got out and followed him. They climbed down into the impression in the ground, but there was no material evidence in sight. "I thought there had to be something here. Something to prove what happened. I—"

Mac's voice cut off. He dropped to his knees with his hands over his ears.

"What is it?" Violeta asked in a panic. "What's wrong?"

"You don't hear that? The ringing?" It was deafening to him, but it wasn't just the noise. Deep in his right ear canal, something moved. Wriggled like an insect that had lodged its way in. "What is that?"

Violeta crouched in front of him, her hands on his shoulders. "Babe, look at me. There's no sound. Nothing's out here but us. We—"

She froze like a mannequin before Mac even saw the beam of light wash over them. It blinded him for a moment, but when his eyes adjusted, he realized the distance between them was increasing. She remained on the ground, but Mac was ascending into the air. He was being pulled into the ship.

Mac's mind flashed back to a moment in the school bathroom the previous week. He had told Bryan he'd do anything to stop any more terrible things from happening to his best friend. He'd said he would trade places if he could. He had meant it then. Even in what could be his final moments, as he was taken away from Violeta by the unearthly beings, he still meant every word of it.

The light faded.

The world around him disappeared.

Suddenly he realized...

He was all alone in the dark.

Direct From the Author

Please visit my website MacheteAndQuill.com, where you'll find signed books, ebooks, and more. Due to the rules of Kindle Unlimited, my ebooks enrolled in that program cannot be sold on my own website. However, the rest of my ebooks as well as signed paperbacks and hardcovers of all my books and stories can be purchased from my website for customers in the US. I like to ship extra goodies such as stickers, coasters, and postcards with all orders. Buying from me directly helps me retain more of the profit, but I truly appreciate purchases made from any retailer you feel most comfortable buying from.

Please also review on Goodreads, Amazon, and Facebook readers groups to get the word out. Finally, please sign up for my newsletter on my site so we can stay in touch. Thank you.

Also by Ryan Hoyt

HORROR AND DARK FICTION

Raventree Hollow

Something evil is feeding off the sins of Raventree Hollow. Shirley Jackson's "The Possibility of Evil" meets Stephen King's *Needful Things* in *Raventree Hollow*, an American gothic horror tale set in the 1950s. A standalone story, it is the first book of the new *A Machete & Quill Horror* line.

We Are Not Alone in the Dark

A high school bully, quarreling friends, and an abusive father are the least of Bryan's worries. When night comes, so do the visitors, and he can't fight back. Who will rescue Bryan if nobody even believes him? A standalone coming-of-age horror novel.

Senior Class: A Raventree Hollow Story

Pearl and Rosemary are the last of their kind. At 90 years old, death calls for them. Who will be the left standing? A short story chapbook set in the town of Raventree Hollow, this can be read as a standalone tale or enjoyed along with *Raventree Hollow*.

Butterscotch: A Raventree Hollow Story

A family moves into an old home to find the previous owner has left behind a hutch with a candy dish. Aggressive neighbors, a trio of cats, and a hidden purple bag lead the family to seek out answers. "Butterscotch" is a short story chapbook set in the town of Raventree Hollow.

Ditch of the Damned

While traveling with her family across the American frontier, Eudora is pulled off the wagon trail by a sensation deep within her bones. She ignores a warning sign and proceeds toward a hole in the earth in the middle of the wilderness. "Ditch of the Damned" is a short story set in 1847, the latest of the A Machete & Quill Horror line.

Freddy Goodman (Ain't No Good Man)

His coming-of-age story was *so* twenty years ago. So why do the words of that old witch still haunt him? A short story of contemporary fiction with elements of magical realism.

EPIC FANTASY

The Forest of Despair

A heroine's first adventure. A kingdom's last hope. The new female-led epic fantasy series The Pierced Shadow Archive begins here.

The Isle of Abandonment

She once saved a kingdom with her friends. Now she must do it alone. Gemma Calvertson's story continues months after the events of *The Forest of Despair* as she and her friends face their biggest challenges yet.

The Realm Beyond

To help her friends and bring truth to the people of Aepistelle, she must join the ranks of her enemy King Davin and his Royal Mystic Committee. Gemma Calvertson's story ends here.

The Witch of Ferathan

An alluring stranger. A trail of destruction. Will Ferathan survive her charm? *The Witch of Ferathan*, a Pierced Shadow Archive novella, is set seventy years before the events of *The Forest of Despair* and can be read as a standalone story.

Acknowledgments

Thank you Mom and Dad for going out of your way to take me to Roswell on the 50th anniversary of the alleged crash there, and for indulging in all my fascinations when I was a kid. I wouldn't have the playful and imaginative mind that allows me to write if you hadn't fostered that in me.

Thanks to the readers who give indie authors a chance, and to the community and admins at Books of Horror on Facebook for creating a place for all of us to share our love.

Thank you to all the folks who helped get this book over the finish line. Beta readers whose feedback shaped the final product or whose encouragement let me know I was on the right track included Trish Wilson, Stephanie Huddle, Emily Casilli, Lisa Breanne, Jessie Bradford, and Kat Guterman.

On the editing front, very special thank you to Amanda DeBord from River Run Editing for your skill and your generosity. I look forward to more projects in the future if you'll have me.

My special edition hardcover is only special because of the hauntingly beautiful stylings of artist Eva Mout.

Anyone that wants to license a piece for a cover, buy a print for your wall, or get inspiration from her lovely dark art should check out her incredible creations at UrsusArt.studio.

The ebook and paperback cover is by Matt Seff Barnes, who I've worked with for five covers now. Matt is an incredible artist whose works inspire me to tell better stories to match his macabre and visionary artwork.

Thank you to author V Castro, who wrote the phrase "we are not alone in the dark" in her book *Goddess of Filth*. I knew as soon as I read it that it'd fit my story perfectly and she replied to my email saying I could use it for my title.

Thanks to my wife Marsha and daughters Natalie and Daisy for allowing me to share my time outside of my day job and other responsibilities with this crazy little hobby of writing. They also encourage and inspire me to keep going when I feel like giving up. They see my tears when my books don't sell, and my joy when things are looking up.

Finally, thank you to my friends and siblings who inspired elements of these characters. I miss so many of my childhood friends. Those were the best days of our lives. I don't want to get in trouble for quoting it, but the last line of the film *Stand By Me* says it best.

Made in United States
Troutdale, OR
02/24/2025